Pierce Feiritear

Illustration by Brian Fitzgerald

First published in 2012 by Pixie Books
21 Cherrymount Park, Phibsboro, Dublin 7, Ireland
www.pixiebooks.ie

ISBN 978-0-9543544-3-5

While the events and some of the characters in this book are based on historic fact,
others are purely fictional.

Editors: Emma Dunne, Gail Quinlan
Typesetting: Artwerk Ltd
Cover illustration (Front): Brian Fitzgerald.
Back: Maria Murray
Graphics: Paul O'Neill, Image Elevation, Joâo Vianey
Cover design: Jason Ellams, Brian Fitzgerald
Printer: Drukarnia Skleniarz

Friday 4 July 1969 was the worst Independence Day ever. We were at the kitchen table eating Mom's chocolate cake when she sprang it on us. Out of the blue.

'Danny, Lucy, I've something to tell you,' she began, smiling brightly.

'Yeah?' I said, through a mouthful of crumbs.

'It's a surprise,' said Mom.

'Yippee!' Lucy screeched – and I mean screeched (you do that when you're only four years old).

'What's the surprise?' I asked.

'Danny, try not to speak with your mouth full,' said Mom. She's always trying to teach us 'manners'.

I swallowed the cake and stared at her. 'So, what's the surprise?'

'We're going on vacation.'

'Yippee!' my sister screeched even louder.

'To Cape Kennedy?' I asked, getting really excited too. *Apollo 11* was going to blast off for the moon on 16 July. It would be amazing to see the launch. And it was only a few hours' drive away. Maybe she'd let my pal Jimmy come …

'No,' she replied.

I tried a second guess. 'Hawaii?' I also loved surfing and dreamed of trying those massive, curling waves. Well, maybe the smaller ones first …

1

Mom shook her head.

'California?' There were good surfing beaches there too.

'No.'

'Where are we going, Mommy?' Lucy's squeaky voice piped up.

Then Mom dropped the bombshell. 'Ireland.'

'What?' I gasped.

'It'll be fun. And you'll finally get to meet your grandparents.'

'Like when?'

'We're flying out Sunday.'

I was stunned. 'This Sunday?'

'Yes.'

'For how long?'

'Three weeks.'

'You're kidding, right?' But I knew she wasn't.

Now don't get me wrong. I have nothing against vacations, Ireland or my grandparents. My mom is Irish. And my dad was too. Her name's Kathleen O'Shea. His was John Joe Sullivan. Can you get more Irish than that? I knew Ireland was a nice place and I wanted to take a vacation there sometime. But not this summer. Not when NASA was about to put a man on the moon. I wanted to stay in Florida, USA, where all the action was going to be.

I had to try and stop this somehow.

'Mom, listen,' I said. 'I can't miss *Apollo 11*. You know I'm doing a school project on it. Everyone in the class is. And you know what the prize is. I want to win. I am *going* to win.'

Our teacher, Mr Walker, is another space fanatic. The first day he walked into the classroom last Fall he was carrying a six-foot-tall model of a Saturn V rocket. Strangely enough, that wasn't the first thing I noticed. I liked his long hair and cool desert jacket. He looked like one of The Beach Boys. *Wow, our new teacher's a hippy,* I thought to myself. *How did he get a job in our school?*

But my attention quickly switched to that rocket. It was a perfect replica.

'What's this and why have I brought it along?' he asked, patting the rocket like it was a horse.

'The Saturn Five,' shouted Bobby Schultz. 'And you've brought it because you'd like a ride to the moon.'

'I sure would,' said Mr Walker. 'Anyone know anything else about it?'

I raised my hand. 'It was designed by Wernher von Braun and it's the most powerful rocket ever built.'

'That's right,' said Mr Walker. 'Anything else?'

'It's got five F-1 engines, at the bottom there,' said Bobby Schultz, pointing at the model.

'Excellent,' said Mr Walker. 'And what's at the top?'

'The command module, of course – where the astronauts are!' Bobby yelped.

'Correct.'

I raised my hand again. 'The Saturn Five stands as tall as a forty-storey building,' I said.

'Three hundred and sixty-three feet to be precise,' said Bobby.

'You're both correct. And why does it need to be so big?' asked the new teacher, smiling broadly.

Bobby's hand shot into the air. So did mine. Mr Walker nodded to me.

'To hold all that fuel you need to burn to get it into space,' I said.

'Good answer, Danny.'

Hey, this guy already knows our names, I thought to myself.

Bobby's hand was still in the air and he was waving it frantically.

Why does Bobby Schultz have to be such a know-it-all? I groaned inwardly.

Mr Walker nodded at him.

'The rocket is liquid propelled,' said Bobby. 'The fuel is liquid hydrogen and liquid oxygen. There's four and a half million pounds of it in there.'

'Well, I can see we've got some space dudes in this class,' said Mr Walker. 'That's what I like to see.'

I might like being in this guy's class, I thought.

And it turned out I did. Everyone did.

Mr Walker's Saturn V rocket stood in the corner of the classroom throughout the year. We followed the Apollo programme all the way, at each step.

In October, *Apollo 7* blasted off from Cape Kennedy and orbited the earth, testing the command module.

In December, *Apollo 8* orbited the moon.

In January, NASA chose the two men who would try to land on the moon: Neil Armstrong and Buzz Aldrin.

In March, *Apollo 9* orbited the earth to test the lunar module.

And in May, *Apollo 10* orbited the moon, again testing the lunar module.

The scene was set for the final countdown to the moon.

'*Apollo 11* has a date with destiny in a few weeks,' Mr Walker told us near the end of the semester. 'Sadly, by that time this school will be closed for summer vacation.' He hung his head, pretending to be sad. 'Aw-w-w-w …'

'Aw-w-w-w …' we all chorused.

'Now, you've all done great work on Apollo this year. It would be a shame to stop now.' He reached into his inside pocket and fished out a white envelope. 'This here is an invitation.' He paused and scanned the class. 'An invitation for four people. Hands up who's been to the Kennedy Space Center?'

Some of us raised our hands.

'Well, if you think this is a regular ol' invitation to a regular visitor tour of Kennedy, you'll be very mistaken. This here is an access-all-areas-special-VIP-meet-the-astronauts-kind-of-invitation ... to the Kennedy Space Center.'

'Wow!' exclaimed Bobby Schultz behind me. I sat up, totally stunned.

'I'm offering this prize to the student with the best project on *Apollo 11*. To arrive on my desk first day next semester. This is a voluntary assignment – repeat, voluntary assignment.'

'Yeah, and I'm going for it,' I whispered to Gloria Fernandez next to me.

'I might too,' she said.

'And whoever takes the prize,' Mr Walker went on, 'can take my Saturn Five there in the corner along with it.'

'Yes!' shouted Bobby Schultz, like he'd already won it.

We'll see about that, I said to myself.

'All right. Who's in for this assignment?' the teacher asked.

A forest of hands shot upwards.

'Good, good,' said Mr Walker.

My best friend, Jimmy Sunn, raised his hand again. 'Can two people do the project together?' he asked.

Mr Walker thought for a moment. 'Okay, I'll allow that. But I'll be expecting a lot more from them.'

I looked over to Jimmy and we gave each other the thumbs up.

This was one competition I sure wanted to win.

I had totally lost interest in that chocolate cake. 'Mom,' I said. 'If I get to win the prize, then you, me, Lucy and Jimmy Sunn get to visit the Kennedy Space Center.'

Mom put her spoon down and looked at me.

'What could be better than that?' I asked. 'We'd get to meet the astronauts, maybe even the *Apollo 11* guys – the scientists. We'll see the launch pad, everything.'

'There's nothing stopping you from doing the project in Ireland, Danny.'

'But Ireland's a million miles from here,' I shouted.

'It's the same distance from the moon as America,' Mom replied calmly. 'The whole world will be watching *Apollo 11*. You can see it on the news in Ireland.'

'But no-one has a TV set over there – you said so yourself.'

Mom laughed. 'I'm sure we'll find one. And if not, there's always the radio. There's also–'

'Please, Mom,' I cut in, 'just please let me stay here.'

'Danny, the tickets are bought. We leave Sunday.'

'Why can't I stay with Aunt Mary in Sarasota?' Aunt Mary is my mom's sister and she's just a couple of hours' drive away. And Sarasota's even closer to Cape Kennedy.

'No, Danny.'

'Why not, Mom?'

'You know why.'

'Please, just this once,' I begged. 'Come on, Mom, be cool.'

But she just looked at me and smiled, a bit tense now.

I knew I was wasting my time.

2

It was my dad who got me interested in rockets. On my seventh birthday he took me to see the John Glenn launch from the Cape. If there's anyone who doesn't know it – and they should! – John Glenn was the first person to orbit earth. Correction: John Glenn was the first *American* to orbit earth. You see, the Russians beat us to that one …

We were living in Chicago at the time. Chicago's not called the Windy City for nothing, and in February it's cold. That trip south seemed to last forever, with Dad and Mom taking turns driving. We had a big old sky-blue automobile that just rattled along. I spent a lot of time asleep in the back – Lucy wasn't born then so I had plenty of room. When we got to Florida I couldn't believe how warm it was. I was back in a T-shirt again.

We stayed in a motel by the sea. I remember it was next to the Banana River, which Dad said was a crazy river full of fish that eat bananas. I believed him and wanted to go see. But Mom said no, there were alligators there.

Dad laughed. 'We only want to stick our toes in the water, don't we, Danny?'

Mom put her foot down, but not in the Banana River. 'John Joseph Sullivan, we are going to the seaside,' she told Dad in that nice bossy way of hers.

Dad just put his hands up like an outlaw caught in the bank, then he grinned. I was cool with that. From what I knew about alligators, I wasn't sticking my toe in any river either, even if it was called 'Banana'.

So we went to the beach instead. Dad and Mom chased each other like kids and had splashing fights in the water. Then Mom lay out in the sun while me and Dad played ball. There were lots of other kids there. The place was jammed. All these people had come for the launch. They were crammed into motels, trailers, even sleeping in their automobiles. Everyone was real friendly, talking about John Glenn's voyage to the stars and how it was about time we caught up with the Russians.

I don't remember much about the vacation, but I'll never forget what happened that Tuesday morning. Dad woke me up early, when it was still dark. 'We've got to hurry, Danny,' he whispered, shaking me urgently. 'They've started the countdown!'

By the time the three of us got to the beach, the sun was a big orange ball over the sea. Already the crowd was there, staring in the same direction. Some were listening to their radios, giving each other thumbs-up signs and saying things like 'All systems are green!' and 'T minus 45 minutes and counting!' We must have been able to see the launch pad from where we were because Dad held me up to look, but I couldn't see much. We hung around for ages, waiting. A couple of us kids started playing together. Before long we were digging this huge hole in the sand.

All of a sudden, I heard whoops and cries. Then I heard this massive – and I mean massive – growling roar, as if the Beast of Doom had just busted out of the ground. But this beast wasn't scaring anyone because people were cheering, waving and jumping like crazy. Dad must have scooped me up, because now I was on his shoulders, staring at this silver tower of smoke shooting into the sky.

'John Glenn's sitting on top of that rocket, Danny!' Dad shouted. My mother blessed herself.

With what looked like the fires of hell spewing out of it, the rocket soared higher and higher, all the time getting smaller and smaller, till soon, very soon, all you could see was a tiny flame shimmering in the sky.

I stared until I could see it no more. Even then I kept staring into that empty blue sky till my neck hurt, marvelling at what I had just seen.

And for the record:

John Glenn's spaceship was called *Friendship 7*.

It lifted off at 9.47 a.m., 20 February 1962.

It flew 100 miles above the ground, at a speed of 17,544 mph.

It orbited earth three times, covering a distance of 75,000 miles in just 4 hours 55 minutes 23 seconds. After all that, it landed safely. Phew!

3

First thing on Saturday morning, I headed over to Jimmy Sunn's house. He was outside trying to fix his bike chain. His hands were covered in grease.

'I've bad news,' I said.

'Huh?'

'Bad news,' I told him.

'You any good at fixing chains, Danny?'

'Listen, Jimmy. My mom's taking Lucy and me to Ireland for three weeks – tomorrow!'

'That don't sound like bad news to me,' said Jimmy, wiping his forehead and leaving a long black smudge. He picked up a screwdriver.

'What about the project?' I asked.

Jimmy looked at me.

'The Apollo project, Jimmy, remember?'

'Of course I remember,' said Jimmy, grimacing as he tried to force the chain back on with the screwdriver.

'Here, put that away,' I said. 'Let me fix it.' I knew I'd probably end up having to fix a lot of our space project too. Jimmy's a great guy, but he needs some … motivating.

I slipped the chain onto the sprocket, spun the wheel around and – hey presto!

'How'd you do that?' said Jimmy.

'Listen, we want to win this trip to the Kennedy Space Center, right?' I continued.

'Hey, I've something to tell you,' Jimmy interrupted.

'I was talking first.'

'Okay, the Kennedy Space Center trip,' said Jimmy, paying attention at last.

'We can win that trip,' I said.

'I want to win the rocket too, Danny.'

'Here's how,' I said. 'I'm going to be away in Ireland but I can write up all the history and background to Apollo – Sputnik, the Russians, John Glenn, Kennedy, the space race, all that kind of stuff. I know it inside out.' It's true, I did.

Jimmy nodded. 'Okay.'

'I'll be away three weeks. There's no TV over there, no newspapers, no nothing. You'll have to look after things on the ground here, Jimmy.'

'Roger.'

'You've got to cover the whole moon landing. Okay?'

'The whole moon landing? You must be kidding!'

'It's as easy as pie,' I assured him. 'All you've got to do is listen to the radio, watch TV, cut out clips from the newspapers and magazines – especially photos – and make notes of everything. I mean *everything*.'

'And you'll write it up for us when you get home?' Jimmy shot back.

'Hey, hold on,' I said.

'You get all the top grades in writing, remember,' added Jimmy with a sly grin.

I thought for a moment. 'Okay, I'll write a lot of it but you've got to help too,' I said.

'It's a deal, buddy,' said Jimmy, giving me a slap on the shoulder.

He pointed a finger towards his house. 'Now follow me, I've something to show you.'

He brought me into the dining room. And, boy, did he have something to show. 'What d'you think of that?' Jimmy asked nonchalantly.

'Wow!' I gasped. Standing there, like a dream from surfing heaven, was a shiny new red and white board.

'It's a Hobie,' said Jimmy. 'You ever heard of Hobart Alter?'

I hadn't. I was new to surfing, unlike Jimmy, whose dad was from Hawaii.

'He's *the* number-one surfboard maker. His board's the Cadillac of the surfing world.'

'When will you try it out?' I asked, trying not to sound jealous.

'We're off to Daytona next weekend.' Jimmy sighed happily.

'Some people have all the luck,' I said.

'Pity you're going away, Danny. You could've come with us.'

'Don't rub it in!' I groaned.

Not only was Jimmy going to Daytona Beach, he was going to his own place in Daytona Beach. His family had an apartment right next to the sea, just off Atlantic Avenue. I had spent two days there during spring break this year. That was the first, and so far the only, time I'd ever tried to surf. Jimmy gave me his board and he used his older brother's.

The great thing about Daytona is that everyone hangs out in their cars on the beach. After breakfast, Jimmy's dad strapped the surfboards to the roof of his Buick and off we went. Florida isn't Hawaii and you can wait a long time for good surf. But that morning the wind was up and those waves looked big enough, even if they were slapping in and breaking too quickly one after the other. Jimmy's dad picked a spot a long way down, and we got ourselves ready.

'It's blown-out and messy out there, boys,' he said as he handed us down the surfboards. 'Danny, we're not going to give you any surfing lessons. Just go out there and do it!'

'That's how I learned anyways,' Jimmy added.

'It's the best way.' His dad smiled.

I felt like a gladiator going into combat as I picked up the board and walked down to the ocean.

The first challenge was to get past where those waves were breaking. We strode out, pushing our boards before us, the cold seeping into our bodies. Then we lay on the boards and paddled. But the sea was so choppy and the waves so higgledy-piggledy, I was quickly dumped and dunked. The same happened to Jimmy. We tried a second time and got turned over again. Back on the beach, Jimmy's dad cheered and laughed. The third time, though, we made it through.

And that was the easy part.

The next step was to catch a wave.

'I'll show you how it's done,' Jimmy shouted. He smiled and crossed his fingers.

I watched as he paddled his board into position. He lay flat, with his back to the waves, looking over his shoulder, waiting for the right one. As a bigger one drew near, he started paddling like crazy and as the wave caught up and lifted his board, he sprang to his feet. Jimmy almost got to stand up with that first try, but the wave tipped him over. His board flew off without him.

There's no point in hanging around, I told myself. *I may as well have a shot too.*

It took some time to paddle into position. My heart thumped as that wall of water came charging towards me. The wave came and I flailed my arms. Suddenly I felt the board lift. But before I could do anything, the torrent of water had moved right on by, leaving me behind.

If at first you don't succeed, try again, I told myself.

I tried again.

This time my timing was better but just as I tried to scramble to my feet the board shot away and I was tossed backwards into the water.

Surfing's not as easy as I thought, I told myself.

But I like a challenge.

I retrieved my board and started over.

Each time I tried to spring up on that surfboard, I either lost my balance or missed the wave or both. By now Jimmy had got the hang of things and was crouched low on his board, riding those crazy waves. He could only ride for a few seconds before the short, quick wave would close over, but he kept his balance and kept sliding in on the foam. It looked so cool.

I gritted my teeth and told myself I was going to get up on that board come hell or high water.

Finally, I did.

It was a big wave, too. A set of waves had come in bigger than all the rest. We paddled out to meet them. I must have been over an hour out there at that point. I let the first one go by. But I caught the second. Suddenly, like a miracle, I was crouching on the board as it lifted. It felt amazing – and terrifying, like riding a wild horse. It felt the way John Glenn might have felt as he was slung off that launch pad. The ride lasted just a second or two, but it seemed like forever.

It ended as suddenly as it had begun, with me crashing head-over-heels into the foam.

I stood and punched the air with my fists.

I was in a bad mood as I strolled home from Jimmy's house. *I want to watch Apollo lift off for the moon. I want to surf with Jimmy at Daytona again. Why do I have to go to Ireland?* I asked myself over and over.

In need of consolation, I stopped at the candy store to buy an ice-cream for myself and some jellybeans for Lucy. As I strolled up the road licking the ice-cream, who did I see getting on his big motorbike outside my house but Mr Walker. It felt weird. It's not every day you see, or want to see, your teacher outside your house, even if he's OK like Mr Walker.

'Am I in some kind of trouble?' I asked, conscious that Mom was standing on the doorstep, eyeing us both.

He flicked up his sunglasses and gave a big grin. 'Now why would you be in trouble, Danny?'

I shrugged and took another lick of my ice-cream.

'You left your NASA booklets behind in class,' Mr Walker said. 'I thought you might need them.'

'Okay, thanks, Mr Walker,' I said.

'Enjoy your vacation,' he said, kicking his black motorbike into action. 'Watch out for those leprechauns!'

With a wave, he was gone.

'Now, up you go and pack your bags, young man,' said Mom. 'We're going to Ireland tomorrow, remember?'

'I know, I know.' I sighed and plodded up the stairs.

'I've left something on the bed for you,' Mom called after me.

'Danny, Danny!' I heard my little sister's voice piping out from the bathroom. 'Come here!'

'In a second,' I replied.

My clothes were in a neat pile on the bed. Perched on top was a new snorkel set and swim fins. It wasn't a surfboard – I was still saving up for that – but it was a cool present all the same.

'Coming, Lucy,' I called.

4

I had never been on an airplane before and my heart was in my mouth as we tore down that runway and took off. But no sooner had we flown through the clouds and levelled off than I began to wonder what all the fuss was about.

Flying's no big deal, I thought.

In fact, it wasn't long before I was bored. And that was just on the flight from Florida to New York. By the time we left there for Ireland, I was an old hand.

Do the astronauts get used to the spaceship too? Might it even get boring after a while? I wondered. *No way! A Saturn V isn't a Boeing 707. Every second during lift off tens of thousands of gallons of fuel are being burned. Sit on top of that beast and you'll really know you're going somewhere! It'll only take the guys four days to get to the moon – if all goes well. Will they be sitting around yawning? I don't think so.*

I took out one of the NASA booklets and started to read – correction: started trying to read. Lucy kept pestering me.

'Are we there yet, Danny?'

'No, Lucy.'

'Will you play I-spy-with-my-little-eye with me, Danny?'

'Later, Lucy.'

'When will we be there?'

'Not for a long while.'

'How long?'

'Six hours.'

'How long is that?'

'Well, you know *The Flintstones*?' (Her favourite cartoon show.)

'Yeah.'

'You'd have to watch *The Flintstones* about twenty times over and by that time you'd be in Ireland.'

'Do you like Barney Rubble, Danny?'

'Yep,' I said.

Mom intervened. 'Your brother's trying to read, Lucy.'

'Do you like Betty, Danny?'

'Yep.'

'And Wilma?'

'Yep.' I waggled the leaflet to show her I was still reading.

'Why don't you draw, sweetie?' said Mom. 'I've nice paper and crayons here.'

'No, don't want to. When are we going to be there, Mommy?'

'Soon,' said Mom.

'Soon when? I'm bored, Mommy.'

See what I mean about planes? Anyway, Lucy eventually fell asleep.

So did I.

Ireland is supposed to be 'forty shades of green', or so Mom had said. But when we arrived it was more like forty shades of wet. It was midday, Monday, the rain was pouring down and it was cold. I don't mean a bit cold. I mean freezing.

'Is it summer here or what?' I asked no-one in particular.

To make matters worse, Lucy, who had just been woken up, started cutting up. And it took ages to collect our bags.

Mom dragged us over to hire an automobile. The lady behind the counter was friendly but her Irish accent was kind of hard to understand. She and Mom started talking about anything and everything – the weather in Ireland, the weather in Florida, about

17

me and Lucy, about the lady's own kids (she had five of them), about shoes and shoe stores and so on and so on …

I thought to myself: *It could be midnight before we get out of here!*

Finally, we got our automobile – a very small one – and set off on the road to Kerry, where my grandparents lived. I stared out at the mist and the grey clouds and the people going by with their umbrellas and wished I was back home in Florida, the Sunshine State.

All of a sudden, I felt bad.

This is where Mom and Dad come from, I thought. *If Dad were alive, he'd be with us right now.*

I figured this trip meant a lot to Mom. She and Dad had grown up not far from each other. She was eighteen when they met. He was a farm boy, one year older. She was supposed to go to college that Fall to train as an elementary school teacher. Instead they ran off together to the United States and got married. Dad worked in construction first, then he joined the Chicago Police Department. Mom worked in a hotel, but when I arrived she gave that up. Later she became a freelance photographer. She still works at that but nowadays she mostly paints (pictures, that is, not houses).

'I'm glad we came here, Mom,' I told her as we drove along the narrow country road.

She caught my eye in the mirror and smiled. 'Do you really mean that, Danny?'

'Yes,' I said, trying to sound like it was true.

Mom gave a happy sigh. 'I'm *so* glad to hear that.'

'I'm really, really glad we're here too, Mommy,' Lucy said. She had been sitting quietly beside me, playing with her dolls.

'No, you're not,' I teased her.

'Am too!'

I started tickling her. 'No, you – are – not!'

'Am too! Am too!' She screeched with laughter. Most kids hate being tickled – I used to hate it – but my sister loves it.

Eventually we crossed an old stone bridge over a river. 'You are now in the Kingdom of Kerry,' Mom declared.

As I gazed out the window I had to admit that what they said about the forty shades of green was true. There was the green of the fields and hills in the distance, of the grass and bushes on either side of the road and of the trees that arched over our heads – mile after mile of dripping-wet green.

Then the road started to rise. Back in Florida we've lots of swamps and the land is flat. Mountains were new to me. And driving up them using a stickshift car was something new to Mom. But pretty soon she got used to it. I was glad of that because there were some crazy bends on that road.

After passing over the mountains and on through some villages, we came to a small town. Mom pulled up outside a hotel on a wide tree-lined street. 'It's three thirty already – you must be starving. Let's eat,' she announced.

The rain had stopped. Mom looked down the street and shook her head. 'If only there wasn't this mist, you'd see such beautiful mountains from here,' she sighed.

'It's good,' I said and shrugged.

'It's good, Mommy,' said Lucy and she shrugged too. 'But I'm hungry.'

We laughed and trooped in to eat.

5

By the time we left the restaurant the sky had brightened and the mist was lifting, uncovering the slopes of the mountains beyond the town. Mom said we should go stretch our legs, so we walked back up the tree-lined street towards the town centre.

'I'm going to get some candy,' I said.

'Can I come too?' asked Lucy.

I shrugged. 'If Mom lets you.'

'Be back here in ten minutes,' said Mom, who had her eye on a clothes store across the street.

With Lucy holding my hand we strolled away. I bought her an ice-cream – a big cone of whipped ice-cream with a stick of chocolate in it and covered in raspberry sauce – then we stopped outside a store called The Kingdom of Curio. Being curious myself, I pushed in the door.

An old man looked up from his newspaper and nodded a greeting. His shop was dark, musty and crammed with old chairs, tables, mirrors, vases, jugs, lots of porcelain figurines of angels, statues of leprechauns and stuff like that. I also spotted some (very dead) butterflies in a glass case, a set of flies (for fishing, that is), a huge sword hanging on the wall, a rock with a fish fossil and various old coins and medals. I picked up an ancient-looking pistol and examined it.

'Are you over from the States?' the man asked softly.

We hadn't spoken a word. How come he knew we were American?

'Yes,' I replied.

'Do you like it here?'

'We've only just arrived,' I said. 'But we're having a good time.'

Suddenly Lucy let out a shriek and grabbed hold of me. The ice-cream toppled off her cone onto my jeans and shoe.

'What are you doing?' I cried out.

She shrank behind me in fear, holding my leg. I turned and saw what had shocked her.

A fox. A glass-eyed, bushy-tailed stuffed fox.

Really, I had to laugh.

The man chuckled too and handed me an old towel. I thanked him and wiped down my jeans. Then I picked up my sister and left.

We drove west out a long and narrow road that skirted the mountains, with the sea below on our right. The sun had peeped out from behind the clouds. Ahead in the distance, I could see another chain of tall mountains.

We sang songs to pass the time. We sang all the ones Lucy knew, like 'Twinkle, Twinkle Little Star', 'Old MacDonald Had a Farm' and 'Rudolph the Red-Nosed Reindeer'. Lucy loved it and as each song finished she shouted, 'Again! Again!'

We were still singing when I caught sight of a beach below us with these great white breakers rolling in.

'Wow!' I hollered. 'You never told me there were surf breaks in Ireland. Take a look at that!'

'I tried to tell you,' said Mom over her shoulder.

'Can we go down there? Just for a look?' I begged.

'Not now,' she replied. 'There are lots of beaches like that around here, believe me.'

My eyes feasted on those waves as we drove past. 'That beats Daytona Beach any day,' I declared. 'I wish Jimmy could see it.'

This vacation was looking better. Okay, I didn't have a surfboard. But I had swim fins, and you could bodysurf with fins any time. People bodysurfed long before they ever thought of surfing with boards.

A while later, we turned onto this crazy mountain road. It was full of holes and only wide enough for one car. Up and up it went, twisting and turning, higher and higher, till we were soon back into the mist. A sheer wall of mountain rose above us; a yawning cliff fell away below – scary! Believe me, it was some white-knuckle ride, because that was the colour of my mom's knuckles as she gripped the steering wheel.

Finally we made it through to the top of the mountain and then it was all downhill into bright sunshine again. We came to a pretty fishing village and Mom said Grandpa's place was only fifteen minutes away.

But five minutes down the road she suddenly pulled up. 'Let's get out, there's something I want to show you,' she said almost in a whisper.

We had come to the crest of yet another hill, part of a long ridge that sloped away on either side. When I got out of the car, I noticed how quiet it was. The breeze was soft on my face.

'Danny, Lucy, take a look down there,' Mom told us. 'This is where we come from, your daddy and I.'

Stretched out below was one of the prettiest sights I had ever seen. A patchwork of tiny green and gold fields ran down to a bay filled with the deepest blue. On the far side of the bay a great headland jutted out into the ocean. Away in the distance another chain of misty mountains rose up.

'It's beautiful,' I said.

'It is surely,' said Mom. She pointed her finger. 'See that

mountain over there that's shaped like a pyramid? Your grandfather's house is just at the foot of it, looking out on that bay. And your daddy's house …' Her voice choked up. She turned and picked Lucy up in her arms.

'What's wrong, Mommy?' Lucy asked.

Mom hugged her. 'Nothing, sweetie.'

We didn't talk much as we drove the rest of the way. It was a short ride anyway. We turned off the road and onto a muddy track that led up to an old farmhouse.

A smile returned to my mom's face. 'At last we're at your grandfather's!'

'Grandpa!' shrieked Lucy.

But where was Grandpa? We knocked on the door and got no reply. We stood around and waited.

'Is there a beach down there?' I asked, looking down at the bay less than a half mile away.

'The most beautiful beach you ever saw,' said Mom.

'Any good waves?'

'You bet.'

We went around to the sheds at the back, thinking he might be there. A gang of tiny yellow chickens scampered around a muddy yard but there was no sign of Grandpa. Lucy went crazy after the chickens, trying to pick one up. But they were way too fast for her.

We went around to the front of the house again.

Mom pointed to the dirt track. 'Over here we call that a bohereen. In Irish that means "little road".'

'Well, there's someone coming up the boher-een,' I said.

A bent figure slowly approached, carrying a heavy sack over his shoulders. Behind him walked a black-and-white sheepdog. We stood and waited. As soon as he saw us, the man slung the bag onto the ground with a thud. It was full of potatoes, I noticed. The dog hung back warily, then slunk away.

23

I felt a bit nervous myself. I had never met my grandfather before and Mom had spoken little about him. After she and Dad ran off to America, they had no contact with each other for a long time. I think that was because her father was angry with her, but there was no sign of that now.

'Well, well, is it yourselves?' his voice sang out. 'Hello, hello!' The way he spoke sounded really funny, like singing. He slapped his hands off each other as if to clean them, but Mom just went over and gave him a hug. 'A hundred thousand welcomes, a hundred thousand welcomes,' he repeated, his blue eyes twinkling just like my mom's do. He turned to Lucy and me. 'And who do we have here now? This big fellow must be Daniel.'

'Your grandson,' said Mom proudly.

He was shaven-headed, lean, of medium build, but his outstretched hand was massive. And when he shook my hand it was a bone crusher.

He turned to my sister, who was holding onto Mom's legs again. 'And this little one is the cut of her mother …'

With that Lucy ran off giggling and disappeared behind the corner of the house.

'That was your granddaughter,' Mom chuckled.

'She's away with the fairies,' he laughed. 'Now, come in and we'll make a cup of tay.'

'What's tay?' I whispered to Mom as we followed him to the door.

She winked at me. 'Tea.'

My grandfather reminded me of Yul Brynner, star of the best cowboy movie ever: *The Magnificent Seven*. True, my granddad was older and wore a pair of farm boots, but everything else about him, the intense eyes, the shaven head, the athletic build, the slow and deliberate manner, even the navy-blue shirt, was just like Yul Brynner in that movie. Real cowboys didn't believe in luxuries.

They led simple, hard lives. If you took one glance around my grandfather's kitchen, from the stone floor to the bare walls to the simple wooden table and rope chairs, you could tell he was the same.

I watched him as he prepared the tea. Mom did all the talking while he filled the kettle with water and set it down on the stove, carefully laid out the cups, saucers, plates, spoons and knives, put out some sugar, butter and milk and cut the brown bread. When the kettle was boiled, he poured the water into a teapot and added three spoons of tea. He covered the teapot with a kind of woollen sweater and set it on the table. It took forever but I didn't mind.

'These kids have never had tea before, John,' said Mom.

'What? Are you pulling my leg?' he said.

'We did have tea, Mommy,' said Lucy.

'You've had iced tea, honey,' said Mom, 'but you've never had real tea like they drink here in Ireland.'

'Iced tay – is that what you drink over in America?' said Grandpa with a look of amazement. 'I've never heard the likes of it!'

'It's so hot over there, you see,' I explained.

He stopped in his tracks and gave me a sudden look. 'Well, I hope you brought the good weather with you!'

I smiled at him. 'It looks like you could do with some sunshine.'

'Stop the lights!' he said with a wave of his hand.

The tea he made was so hot it burned my lips and I had to add a lot of extra milk to it. This Irish tea tasted, well, different.

After that, I slipped outside to have another look around.

I went over to the sack of potatoes he had left in the yard and tried to lift it. Impossible. *That old guy is strong*, I thought to myself.

I went back to the sheds. One was being used as a chicken house and was full of those little yellow guys and their nervous clucking mothers. The shed next to it held old pieces of rusted farm equipment. But the third one, the biggest, was packed full of timber. The sight of all those planks of wood set me thinking.

Perhaps one of these would make a surfboard, I told myself.

I continued with my tour.

The door of the last shed was open but when I saw the sheepdog eyeing me from the corner I did a U-turn and skipped back down to the house. Mom was taking our bags from the car. 'Come on, Danny, shoulder to the wheel,' she commanded.

I gave her a salute. 'Yes, Ma'm.'

A steep and creaking stairs led up to four tiny bedrooms. I moved into one at the front of the house, and Mom and Lucy shared the room opposite. Our beds were made of brass with funny knobs on the end and looked ancient. By the time we had unpacked it was almost dark outside. Lucy climbed into bed and I told her her favourite story, *Goldilocks and the Three Bears*. She must have been really tired because she fell asleep halfway through it.

I decided to call it a day too. When I switched off the light, the total darkness was spooky and the silence even spookier. There were no street lights in this part of the world and no cars passing by.

After a while I heard Mom coming up the stairs and going to her room. I lay there but could not sleep. Mom couldn't sleep either, because I could hear her shifting about on that creaking brass bed. I wondered what she was thinking – not sad thoughts, I hoped.

It felt strange here, like being on another planet.

6

Did you ever wake up in a place and not know where you were? It was like that on my first morning in Kerry. I stared at the ceiling for a while, yawning, in a kind of a trance. It was early, seven o'clock. I could hear my grandfather moving around downstairs – I knew it was him from the sound of his clumping boots. Outside all was quiet, except that every now and then this rattling sound rose up and faded away as if a stagecoach was heading down the road.

I got up and pulled back the curtain. Sheep grazed in the field outside. The day was sunny and clear. Over on the right a huge mountain peak soared above the rest into the cloudless sky. I hadn't noticed it the day before, as it must have been shrouded in mist. Beyond the fields, the blue sea looked very inviting. I decided I'd investigate right after breakfast. As I dressed I heard the rattling outside again. I looked out and saw a farmer driving a horse and cart along the road.

I peeped in on Mom and Lucy. They were still asleep, my sister hugging her teddy bear as always.

Down the creaking stairs I went and into the kitchen. My grandfather was standing by the window, shaving with this deadly-looking cut-throat razor, just like you see in the cowboy movies. He gestured for me to sit down. 'There's a fresh pot of tay there. Pour yourself a cup.'

'That's a sharp blade,' I remarked.

'You need a steady hand, boy,' he replied, 'a steady hand.'

As I poured the tea into one of the enormous mugs on the table he gestured with the blade towards the loaf of brown bread on the table. 'Now, cut yourself a slice. I baked it myself.'

'Cool,' I said. I cut myself a thick slice and buttered it.

'There must be great excitement in America these days,' said my grandfather.

'You mean the moon landing?' I said.

'Aye, the landing on the moon,' he said. 'Do you really think they're going there?'

'Sure.'

He lowered the blade and turned to me. 'But are they really going to the moon? In all seriousness?'

'Sure!'

'You think so? I have my doubts,' he said. 'I have my doubts.'

'Are you serious?' I could see he was, or at least I thought he was.

'The moon is an eternity away. How could you fly there? And how could you put a man there? And fly back again? It can't be done, I tell you!'

'It can and it will,' I insisted.

'How do you know that? They could be pulling your leg!'

'You're kidding,' I said.

'They are pulling your leg, boy!'

'You're the one pulling my leg.' I laughed.

He smiled and wiped his face with a towel. Then he turned to me again. 'Do you like my bread?'

'I love it,' I said. I meant it too.

'The proof of the pudding is in the eating,' he said. 'And the same applies to anyone who says he's going to the moon.'

I didn't argue the point with him.

Mom and Lucy still hadn't appeared, so after my breakfast I set off for the beach.

As I strolled down the bohereen I heard this humming sound, as if a plane was circling somewhere above. It took a few moments to figure out what it was – bees, lots of honeybees, buzzing and humming among the red and purple flowers on the bushes. I was wary of those little buzzers. What if they all suddenly decided to attack? You wouldn't stand a chance.

I turned onto the road and met a farmer with his horse and cart rattling along. The two huge wheels had no tyres, which explained where all the noise was coming from. The cart was carrying a metal cylinder shaped like a huge chess pawn. The farmer was dressed just like my granddad, except that he wore a cloth cap. He nodded in a friendly way, greeting me in Irish as he went by. At least I figured it was Irish because it sure sounded strange. Mom said that this part of Kerry was one of the few places left in Ireland where they still spoke the old language.

Leaving the road, I followed a track down to the beach. And what a beach it was – a half-mile crescent of white sand washed by Atlantic blue. Calm waves rolled in, broke with a low rumble and raced up the shore towards you, whispering and hissing, only to retreat just as speedily. I strolled along taking it all in. There was no-one there. Not even a footprint.

I was a beginner at surfing but I could tell those waves were good. They were smooth and well-formed, yet big enough to pick you up and take you for a ride. All I needed to do was make the surfboard. If I found the right piece of wood in Grandpa's shed and got my hands on a saw and plane, I was sure I could do it. It wasn't exactly rocket science. Jimmy's dad had made his own board as a kid in Hawaii.

At the end of the beach stood an outcrop of rock. I crossed this and found myself on another smaller beach. I walked over this and soon I was on a bohereen that wound by yet another sandy cove and then on past some farmhouses before linking up with the main road. I decided to follow it back to my grandfather's place.

It was so quiet on that country road, something I wasn't used to at all. You could hear the sudden chirping of a bird, the humming of bees and the breeze sifting through the long grasses. As I strolled along in the warm sunshine I kept looking over my shoulder, expecting an automobile to race around the bend. None came.

Something else did, though.

It started with the distant rattle of cartwheels. *Some farmer on his way to the creamery*, I thought.

The noise ebbed and flowed as it hit this bend and that on the road, but steadily grew louder. Whoever he was, he was in a hurry.

I still couldn't see much because of the high green ditches on either side of the road but soon I could hear the rapid clip-clop-clip of his horse and, boy, was he driving that animal. Suddenly the horse and cart came thundering around the bend. I stepped back into the ditch.

The horse, a rich dark brown with white socks, was young and powerful and moving like the wind.

And the farmer was no farmer at all but a girl, about my own age, in a sky-blue summer dress. She wasn't sitting either but standing right up on the cart. With the reins in her hand, her brown hair flowing in the breeze, she looked like a charioteer from Ancient Rome.

And she was pretty.

She nodded to me as she passed, which was cool considering the speed she was going.

I turned to look as she flew by.

7

Lucy had lost no time in making friends with the sheepdog. When I came up the bohereen they were in the yard playing fetch. Still in her pyjamas, she was in a state of high excitement, holding a tennis ball above her head. The dog stood ready to pounce, eyes fixed on the ball.

'Danny, Danny, watch this. He's really fun.' Squealing with delight, she tossed the ball about as far as a four-year-old can. 'Go get, Kerry, go get!'

The dog pounced on the ball – seizing it after one bounce – then dropped it at her feet. 'Good boy, Kerry, good boy!' She stroked his shaggy black-and-white coat and threw the ball again. She turned to me with a big smile. 'His name is Kerry.'

'I see,' I said. *A funny kind of name*, I thought. *A bit like us calling our dog Florida … But then who are we to talk? We named our dog Bonzo.*

Then Grandpa came round the corner of the house with a hedge shears in his hand. He issued a short command in Irish. Immediately Kerry dropped the ball and sat down, awaiting further instructions.

'Would you like to give the lamb his breakfast?' Grandpa asked Lucy.

'What lamb?' said Lucy.

'The little lamb in the field below,' he said. 'I've to bring him his breakfast every morning. And his dinner and supper. D'you want to feed him?'

My sister gave a little shrug of her shoulders. 'Okay, Grandpa.'

'Righty-o, I'll go fetch his bottle.'

'Are you serious?' I asked.

'The mother died in the spring. I've been looking after the little one since,' he said.

So Grandpa's got a pet. I smiled to myself.

I took Lucy by the hand and we walked over to the gate. There were about forty sheep and lambs in the field, eating grass and enjoying the sun. I couldn't tell one from the other.

Presently our grandfather came out with what looked like a giant baby's bottle full of milk. Lucy cheered.

'How do you know which lamb it is?' I asked.

'I call him.'

'What's his name?' asked Lucy.

He took off his cap and scratched his head. 'Well, I don't … I just call him. I suppose you could say I call him Hello,' he said, with that twinkle in his eye. He held out the bottle to my sister. 'Now, if you want to feed him, hold onto that.'

Lucy grabbed the bottle with both hands.

Grandpa cupped his hands around his mouth. 'Hel-lo! Hel-lo!' his voice sang out.

Out of the forty heads, one suddenly shot up and looked our way. At once the lamb came hurrying towards us. The rest of them didn't pay one bit of attention.

'Now hold that bottle tight,' I told my sister. It was so big and heavy I had to help her with it. Lucy had gone very quiet.

In an instant the lamb latched onto the bottle. His little tail wagged as he sucked and, believe me, in ten seconds he had drunk every drop.

'Wow!' I gasped. 'That is one thirsty lamb.'

'And do you think he'd thank you?' said Grandpa. 'That fellow has no gratitude.'

True – Hello was already running back to his friends.

'No gratitude!' my grandfather roared at the retreating lamb.

Just then I heard the sound of cartwheels from the road.

'The wild one's on her way back from the creamery,' said Grandpa with a nod of his head.

Over the top of the ditch I saw the head of a horse flying along and the girl flying along after it. It was like something out of the Kentucky Derby.

'Do they have girls like that in America?' he asked with a twinkle in his eye.

'Out in the Wild West,' I replied. 'Who is she?'

'Eilis Baker, Pat Baker's daughter. That's their place over there,' he said, pointing to a farmhouse across the fields. 'Good people.' Then he chuckled. 'She's some lassie.'

Approaching the bend, she reined in her horse. A moment later they turned off the road and disappeared from view.

That horse has earned his breakfast, I thought to myself.

Speaking of which, the delicious smell of sausages being cooked was now wafting out from the kitchen. Suddenly I felt hungry.

Mom was making us what she called a full Irish breakfast: sausages, bacon, fried egg, broiled tomato and blood sausage, which they call 'black pudding' over here (I ate everything except that.) After such a huge breakfast, I wanted to lie down somewhere!

But I had a plan for the day … starting with that surfboard.

'I need a piece of wood, sir,' I told Grandpa as I cleared away the dishes. 'Is it okay if I take some from your shed out there?'

'Work away,' he replied.

Mom laughed. 'Danny, what you're calling a shed is the house your grandfather was born in.'

I looked at him. 'She's kidding, right?'

Grandpa just gave a little smile.

'Six of them were born and raised in that house,' added Mom.

'Wow,' I gasped. 'I'm sorry I called it a shed.'

'No need to apologise. And what do you need the wood for?' he asked.

'A surfboard.'

'And what's that?'

I explained what it was.

He seemed puzzled. 'Is it some class of a boat you're making?'

'Something like that,' I said.

'A kind of boat you've never seen in Kerry before,' said Mom.

He told me I could take all the wood and tools I needed.

So I went out to the, eh, house.

Inside it was dark but as dry as a bone. I left the door open so I could see. Dozens of planks and boards were stacked up against the wall. I needed something wide enough, thick enough, long enough and yet light. Jimmy's board was about ten foot, but I'd read that many surfers these days were riding shorter boards of about six and seven foot. Of course, these were hollow, state-of-the-art boards. I didn't think I should make mine that short.

I remembered what Jimmy's dad had told me about surfing in Hawaii as a kid. 'You could surf on just about any piece of wood if it's the right shape,' he had said. 'One of the kids I hung out with surfed on his mom's old ironing board – he used to fly on it.'

Most of Grandpa's planks were too narrow, but I turned up two that were the right width. I took one outside and laid it on the ground.

Then I went to my bedroom and fetched my *International Surfing* magazine, a pencil, ruler, eraser and some of the paper I'd brought for the space project. First, I measured the plank. It was ten foot by one and a half. I drew a line and sawed it back to nine foot.

Next, to get the shape right. I looked at pictures in the magazine and practised drawing on paper. I had to get the nose and tail right, to make them rounded enough. Rounded seemed better than pointed in case the board hit me in the water.

When I had the shape right on paper, I outlined it with pencil on the board. All I needed to do now was cut it with the saw.

But that was easier said than done, especially when you're trying to saw on a curve. I was glad when Grandpa arrived on the scene and offered to help.

Despite his sixty-three years, Grandpa worked like Superman. He cut deftly through that wood, resting the plank on a small table. Then he rounded off the nose and tail with the confidence of a carpenter.

'Are you going to get up on that in the water?' he asked, raising his eyebrows again.

'That's the plan,' I replied.

'And sail the waves with it?'

'Yep.' I smiled.

'You're as mad as those astronauts so,' he said. And with that he strolled away.

8

My surfboard was ready but I didn't try it out that day. Instead I went swimming, which was some experience. The water was fr-ee-ee-zing. I could only stay in it about ten minutes. The waves were great and I bodysurfed some, swam some, bodysurfed some more and then ran all the way up the beach to get warm again. No-one was there except one other family and us – and this was supposed to be the vacation season.

Grandpa had dinner ready for us when we got back: a big pot of potatoes cooked in their skins and another pot full of carrots. He served up fish with it. The fish was called mackerel, which I'd never seen or tasted before.

After dinner Mom said she wanted us to visit some of our relations. 'Aw, Mom,' I protested.

'I'm tired too, Mommy,' Lucy whined.

Mom sighed a big *okay* and agreed to put off seeing her cousin till the following day.

I wondered when we were going to see my dad's mom and dad, because I thought if we were going to visit anyone they should come first. But I guess there must have been problems with them as well back then. You know, the way Mom and Dad had *eloped to America* and all that. Mom had to be feeling nervous about seeing them.

Anyway, tired as I was that evening, I picked up my pen and started on the space project. If I didn't get something done in Ireland I could forget it.

I wrote down the heading 'Rockets'.

Then I drew a picture of one below it.

Next I flicked through my papers and stuff looking for a photo of a certain Mister Robert H. Goddard. The Chinese may have invented rockets a thousand years ago, but the person who kick-started the whole business, the man who put the R in Rocket, was Robert.

He came up with two incredible ideas:

1. Instead of putting powder in your rocket, he asked, why not use liquid fuel? It's more efficient and a lot safer. He advised using liquid hydrogen as the fuel and liquid oxygen as the oxidiser.
2. If you want to go into space, said Robert, you'll need a multi-stage rocket. Think about it – you won't escape the pull of earth's gravity unless you jettison your tanks after you burn up all that fuel.

It was tough being a young genius back in the early 1900s in Massachusetts. They laughed when Robert said people would fly to the moon one day. And they sniggered when he built himself a rocket.

One icy day, on 16 March in 1926, Robert put his rocket into his car and drove to his Aunt Effie's farm. He called his rocket *Nell.* She stood ten feet tall. He set her up in a field, well away from his auntie's house.

A friend volunteered to light the thing with a blowtorch. The friend was smart enough to tie the blowtorch to a long stick – a very long stick.

For one horrible moment, nothing happened. *Nell* just sat there.

Then … *KAZOOM!* She shot skywards.

Nell flew 41 feet into the air and landed 184 feet away in a cabbage patch.

It was a two-and-a half-second flight. Not bad for a beginner.

He kept working at it and sent up another rocket. This one came down with such a bang that the police were called. The local newspaper headlines mocked him: MOON ROCKET MISSES TARGET BY 238,799½ MILES!

It's the ½ mile part that really hurts. I think the sneering and the jeering really got to him this time because he moved away, down to the desert in New Mexico. Besides, it was safer there for testing rockets.

By the 1930s Robert was designing rockets that moved faster than the speed of sound and flew 9,000 feet into the sky. That's when things began to get scary…

I had just finished a page on Robert and was starting on another guy called Werhner von Braun, who had built rockets in Florida for the National Aeronautics and Space Administration (NASA) after World War Two. Then I heard voices outside. Visitors.

The voices surged into the house and I could hear another woman getting all excited in the kitchen. Then Mom called me from the foot of the stairs.

'In a minute,' I yelled.

'Danny, where are you? Come on down!'

If you can't beat them, join them, I thought, tossing my pen and notebook aside.

When I shuffled into the kitchen I saw this lady, a little older than Mom. Two kids were with her. One was a boy, about ten, with a smiling face full of freckles. The other was peering out the window with Grandpa.

It was a girl – correction: the girl.

'Nora, this is my son, Danny,' Mom introduced me.

The lady smiled and shook my hand. She introduced me to her son. His name was Sean. Then she called her daughter. 'Eilis, will you come over here and shake the hand of a boy from America?'

The girl turned from the window. Her eyes were brown and very pretty. Her hair was down to her shoulders.

'Hi, I'm Danny,' I said.

She smiled and said, 'Pleased to meet you.' She went back to the window.

'Eilis! There must be something fierce interesting out there for you to be turning your back on a handsome boy like that!' Her mother laughed. Mom laughed too, and winked at me.

'It's the fox we're looking at,' my grandfather explained.

I stepped over and peered out into the twilight.

'She's over there on the ditch. And up to no good, I can tell you,' Grandpa muttered.

I couldn't see anything.

'She took two lambs on me in the spring,' he added bitterly.

'How do you know it was the fox?' the girl asked him. 'Might have been a stoat.'

'No. 'Twas the vixen.'

'She's away,' the girl said suddenly.

Red fur flashed across the ditch half-way down the field. I'd never seen a live fox before and this one slipped away like a thief.

'I'll have to deal with her,' said Grandpa grimly.

'What do you mean?' she quizzed him. 'You're not going to harm her, are you?'

Grandpa was silent.

'Now, sit down, Nora, and I'll make a pot of tea,' said Mom, changing the subject.

'No, no, it's too late, we only dropped by to say hello,' the woman insisted. 'Come down to us tomorrow morning, Kathleen, and we'll have a proper chat.'

'Surely,' said Mom.

'And you'll come down too, won't you?' Nora asked me. 'Have you ever milked a cow?'

I shook my head dumbly.

'Well, there you are now,' she said, as if she'd just discovered a hugely important piece of information.

'He's always wanted to be a cowboy,' said Mom, smiling.

'He's come to the right place so,' the woman replied.

9

The minute my head hit the pillow I was out like a light.

Being tired won't stop you from having dreams and I was woken by a freaky one. I was walking along a beach with a surfboard. The waves were spectacular: I just had to try and catch one. Next thing I'm paddling on the board and this wave, the biggest wave ever, is rearing up. It's *perpendicular*, the size of a house, and I've just sprung up on my board when I notice the beach has disappeared and in its place there's these jagged rocks – I'm going to be dashed to pieces against them!

End of dream.

Is it any wonder I woke up?

I lay there hoping I'd drift back to sleep. The window was open and I became aware of a sound, a slow rumbling roar.

I got out of bed and pulled back the curtain.

The sheep were still huddled together in the middle of the darkened field, all pale and ghostlike. Beyond, in the field across the road, I spotted an outcrop of rock that I hadn't noticed earlier. The mountains were silhouetted against the night sky. Everything was peaceful and still but for that noise. What was it?

It was only when I stuck my head out the window that it dawned on me. It was the sound of the sea.

I tiptoed down the creaking stairs for a glass of water. On my return, I paused on the landing where a bright sliver of the moon lit up the back window. I stood gazing up at it. It was amazing to think that while earth hurtled through space at 67,000 mph and

41

simultaneously spun at 1,000 mph, we could fire a rocket at another moving target so far away and hit the right spot.

Those three astronauts sure were brave. I wondered how they felt right now.

Then a picture of Mr Walker limping along the school corridor floated into my mind. I'd been weeks in his class and hadn't noticed anything unusual about the way he walked until Jimmy mentioned it at recess one day.

'Where do you think he got the limp?' he asked me.

'Who?'

'Mr Walker.'

'No way.'

'Has so. Where d'you think he got it?'

'Limp? I need to check this out,' I said.

And I did, two minutes later when he passed down the corridor. To my surprise, he had a slight yet suddenly noticeable limp in his right leg. 'Fancy that, you're right,' I said to Jimmy. 'Where'd he get it?'

'I'm asking *you*.'

I shrugged. 'Search me.'

We strolled into the classroom. 'Danny's only just picked up on Mr Walker's limp,' Jimmy called out to everyone. 'And he wants to know how he got it. Anyone know?'

'Probably came off his motorbike,' said Kate.

'I'd say so too,' Linda agreed.

'Nah, he blew off his big toe in one of his science experiments,' Tom Ritchie said and we all laughed.

'You're wrong, actually,' spoke a voice from the back of the class. It was Bobby Schultz. Everyone turned around.

'Mr Walker was in 'Nam,' said Bobby. He said no more than that.

He didn't have to. The smiles faded from our faces. We all knew Bobby's big brother was over in Vietnam, putting his life on the line for his country.

Mr Walker had done the same thing. And in two weeks' time those astronauts would as well.

10

I woke up with Lucy jumping on my bed. 'Wake up, wake up, you sleepy head!' she sang, her blue eyes smiling down at me. With her thick red hair bobbing as she jumped she looked more like a pixie than ever.

I closed my eyes again, pretending I was back asleep.

'Wake up, sleepy head! Wake up, wake up, get out of bed!' She kept on singing and bouncing.

It was time to play Zombies. It's a cool game and it scares the living daylights out of my sister, but she loves it too.

'*Uhhhh*,' I moaned deeply. Lucy stopped singing.

I opened my eyes and stared straight ahead. She stopped jumping.

I suddenly sat up in bed. She screamed.

I stretched out my arms and waggled my fingers, ever so slowly. She hopped off the bed and ran from the room. But I wasn't finished, not by a long shot.

Hunching up one shoulder, dragging one foot along, I slowly started down the stairs after her. '*Uhhh laaalaa.*'

'Mommy! Mommy!' Lucy screeched, both terrified and delighted.

'Oh no!' cried Mom in mock horror.

By now Lucy was clutching Mom's legs in the kitchen and as I stumbled towards her, staring and moaning, she fled into the garden. I followed her, calling gently. 'Come on back, Lucy. I'm only kidding.'

44

She was peeping at me round the corner of the house. Just as she plucked up the courage and edged towards me I pounced again. Well, the shrieks out of her as I turned back into a 'Zombie' and grabbed her. That's how the game ends each time.

'Can we play Zombies again, Danny?' she asked straight away.

'Before you do,' Mom called out from the kitchen, 'please fetch some eggs from the hen house. I'll fry you some, sunny side up.'

'Sounds good,' I answered, taking my sister by the hand. 'Come on, let's go to the chickens.'

I must have overslept because the sun was already high in a cloudless sky. Still in my bare feet, I carefully picked my way on tufts of grass in the farmyard. A couple of hens and chicks scurried out the door as soon we entered. It was dark in there, and you could just make out the bare stone walls and the straw on the ground, then an old plough and a greenish bridle hanging from a nail.

'It's smelly in here,' Lucy complained.

'It's the chickens,' I said. 'Let's find us some eggs.'

The hens had laid their eggs in the straw and we gathered six in no time. Some of them were still warm. I gave two to Lucy to carry and we headed back to the house.

We met our grandfather coming through the yard with a big ladder over his shoulder. He winked at us.

'Can I give Hello his bottle?' Lucy wanted to know.

'You can surely, after your breakfast.' He saw the eggs in our hands. 'If you visit the hens in the evening won't you make sure to lock the door after you?' he said.

'Yes, sir,' I replied. 'Do you want me to lock it now?'

'No, only in the evening. I always keep it locked – in case the fox comes.'

'I'll remember that,' I told him.

Those fresh fried eggs were delicious. But no sooner had I

wolfed two of them down than Mom had more work for me. 'We're out of milk, Danny. You can go down to the village for some. Take your grandfather's bike.'

'I was going to work on my surfboard,' I wailed.

'You can do that later. And remember, we're visiting the Bakers this morning,' said Mom.

'But–'

She gave me one of her looks. 'No "buts", sonny. Now get on that bike and fetch us the milk!'

I couldn't believe it when I went outside. Grandpa was standing on top of the roof like a trapeze artist on a high wire. The man had to be crazy, because the slope on the roof was like that on Mount Everest. He must have climbed the big ladder resting against the wall and set a smaller ladder on the roof itself. Sixty-three years of age …

'What are you doing up there?' I enquired.

'It's them blasted jackdaws and their nest!' he called down.

I watched as he stuck his arm into the chimney pot.

'I hope Mom doesn't see you up there,' I said.

All of a sudden a great ball of twigs landed on the ground beside me. I was appalled to see an egg in the nest. It had survived the fall intact. 'There's an egg in it!' I shouted.

Now he had taken up a broom handle with a hook in it and was using it to pull up more material from the chimney.

'There's an egg in the nest!' I yelled again.

'There's a what?'

'*An egg!*'

He looked down at me and smiled. 'Will you have it for breakfast?'

I didn't think that was funny.

I stepped back as another clump of the nest came tumbling down. *Grandpa has a tough streak. I pity that fox if he ever finds her.*

Yet he had treated that lamb so kindly. It was hard to figure the man out.

More twigs and bits of straw came flying. I stepped back in and retrieved the egg. It was pale blue, speckled with black and grey, perfect as a jewel. But stone-cold.

'Can I borrow your bike, Grandpa?' I hollered.

'Take it any time you want, boy,' he said. He looked at the piles of twigs scattered all over the garden, shook his head and muttered something in Irish.

Grandpa's bicycle was a great big black thing with massive wheels and mudguards and a crossbar so high you could barely touch the pedals. I had to cycle standing up.

It was a nice ride to the village with the sun on my back, the soft sea breeze on my face. Swallows flitted across the road ahead of me and there wasn't a car in sight. I found myself thinking how different it was from Florida: no phone, no refrigerator, no record player, sofa, shower or even a carpet. Then it hit me: *I've got to find a TV before Apollo 11 takes off!*

The village was like something out of the Wild West. A one-horse street nestled at the foot of the mountain. It had a church, a school house, one or two small stores, a couple of saloons and the sheriff's office (which my Mom had called the guards' barracks). Outside one of the stores stood a horse and cart, minus its driver, the horse waiting patiently. Two children sat on a seat, licking popsicles, their mom sitting opposite in a car with the door open, doing the same. They were on vacation, I figured. The lady in the store greeted me in Irish when I entered.

'*Dia dhuit,*' (Dee-a gwit) she said.

This time I was able to reply, because my mom had taught me the previous night.

'*Dia's Muire dhuit,*' ('Dee-a iss Murra gwit) I replied. Basically, it means 'May God be with you.'

47

I asked for the milk.

'Are you staying back at John O'Shea's?' she asked.

'I am.' *How does she know?* I wondered.

'So you must be Kathleen's boy?'

I nodded.

'I went to school with your mother. And your father, Lord rest him,' she said softly. 'In that very school out there.'

'Really?'

'You've a great look of him.'

'So they say,' I replied.

'He was a fine man, a fine, fine man …' Her voice trailed off.

'Yes,' I said, shuffling uncomfortably.

She gave me the milk and my change. 'Are you staying long?'

'Three weeks.'

'Tell your mother to drop in to see me,' she said as she picked up two candy bars and handed them to me. 'This one's for you, and the other's for your little sister.'

I thanked her. *This lady seems to know everything about us*, I thought.

'Have you seen any of our film stars yet?' she asked as I turned to leave.

I shook my head.

'Hollywood has come to West Kerry,' she declared proudly, 'to make a big film!'

'Like a movie?'

'A movie – that's what you call it,' she said with a smile. 'You've heard of Robert Mitchum, haven't you? He was in my shop last Saturday.'

'No kidding!' Robert Mitchum is one of the coolest movie stars ever. I loved him in *The Longest Day*, which is one great war movie.

'Standing right where you are now. He bought the newspaper

48

from me,' she continued. '"Ma'm, you wouldn't have today's *New York Times* by any chance?" he asked me, half joking, like. "No, only *The Irish Press*," I said. "And it's yesterday's," I told him. "I'm afraid today's paper hasn't come in yet." "I'll take it," says he with a big grin. And he slaps a pound on the counter – and not a penny change would he take! I have it up there,' she said, pointing to the shelf where the large green banknote was pinned. 'And there it shall remain.'

'He's a great movie star,' I said.

'And a real man,' she said.

Robert Mitchum plays US general Norman Cota in that movie. The general was pinned down with his men on Omaha Beach in Normandy on D-Day, 6 June 1944. Nazi gunfire had cut down thousands of soldiers on that small stretch of sand. Withdrawal and defeat were staring them in the face. 'Hell no, we're not leaving,' General Cota announced. 'We're going up that hill!' As bombs and bullets rained down, he got to his feet and walked up and down rallying his men. 'There's only two types of men gonna stay on this beach,' he shouted, 'those who are already dead and those who are going to die … So listen to me, all of you, we've got to get out of here!'

Did they get off the beach? You bet they did!

Of course, Mitchum was just an actor playing a part. General Cota did it for real, like Bobby Schultz's brother and Mr Walker.

I remembered telling Mom about my teacher. 'Guess what I heard at school today?' I had said, strolling into the kitchen. 'Mister Walker was in Vietnam.'

'In the Marine Corps,' said Mom, who was peeling carrots at the sink.

'How did you know?'

'He was awarded the Purple Heart.'

'Where did you hear all this?'

'I'm in the Parent-Teacher Association, aren't I?'

'Why didn't you tell me?'

'You students don't have to know everything, do you? He's not a soldier now. He's a teacher.'

'Yeah, but why keep it a secret?'

'Who said it was a secret?'

'Well, I didn't know, and no-one in my class knew – only Bobby Schultz.'

'I think you know your teacher by now, Danny. He's not the kind who brags about things.'

'Maybe he's keeping his head down because of all the anti-war protests,' I said. Every other night you'd switch on the TV and see coverage of some protest against the war in Vietnam.

'I don't think so,' said Mom.

'Or then again,' I said, 'maybe he's an anti-war guy himself, you know, with the long hair and all that.' It was true, some of the protesters were ex-soldiers who had fought in Vietnam.

'Danny,' Mom had said, putting down the peeler. 'Just because you've got long hair doesn't make you an anti-war protester. Does it?'

Still in a daydream, I stopped at the schoolhouse on my way home. So this was where my mom and dad went to school.

It was an elementary school with just two classrooms and was run-down. A closer look told me it was shut down, period. The gate was rusted and hanging off its hinges, the tiny yard was choked with weeds, some slates were missing on the roof and paint was peeling off the window frames. I tried to imagine what it had been like when my parents were running around here as kids. Weird.

I was going to take a closer look, but when I pulled the gate open and walked into that yard, I felt … I felt like I couldn't go any further. There's something sad, something spooky, about an abandoned school, and this one especially. I didn't need to see any more.

I hurried to Grandpa's bike and cycled away.

11

'You must've brought the good weather with you!' Mrs Baker greeted us at the door of her house.

'It's a fine day, Nora,' said Mom.

Which is why I want to go surfing, I thought.

'Himself has been cutting the hay since early morning,' said Mrs Baker.

'Isn't he the wise man, making hay while the sun shines,' said Mom.

'Come in, come in,' Mrs Baker said. 'And we'll put the kettle on.'

It's funny. People were always talking about the weather and drinking endless cups of tea in Ireland.

A smell of baking wafted through the kitchen. No sooner had Mrs Baker seated us at the table than she whipped out a tray of golden, lumpy cakes from the stove. 'Now, who would like a hot scone?' she enquired, looking straight at me.

'I'll try one,' I volunteered.

'I'll try one,' echoed Lucy.

'Me too,' said Mrs Baker's son, Sean, strolling into the kitchen.

'And where's your sister?' his mother asked.

'In the field below with Dad.'

'Go get her,' she commanded.

I wolfed down the hot scones with homemade blackberry jam – it was delicious (and the blackberries were picked right off the hillside). I had almost finished mine when Sean came back with his sister. They sat down and helped themselves to the scones.

Sean started firing questions at me. 'Do you watch *Mission: Impossible* in America?'

'Sure do. Do you have it here?'

'I watch it all the time. D'you like it?'

'Yeah.' *So the Bakers have a TV set*, I thought.

A broad grin spread across his face. 'Would you like to play it?'

'Maybe,' I said.

'And what about *The Man from U.N.C.L.E.*? D'you like that too?' asked Sean.

'Sean, you'll have the poor lad killed with all your questions,' his mom cut in. 'Eilis, why don't you and Sean show our visitors the farm?'

'Would you like to have a look?' the girl asked me.

'Sure, why not,' I said.

Eilis took Lucy by the hand and out we went.

We walked in silence for a bit. Then I asked about the size of the farm and Eilis pointed out the boundary walls, which ran in a long strip from the top of the hill down to the sea.

'Would you like to see our cows?' she asked my sister, who nodded happily. But the cows were at the far end of the field.

'Cows are very curious animals,' said Eilis as she climbed over the gate. 'Wait and I'll show you.'

I wondered what she was going to do – call them? Or drive them up to us? Instead she walked out a few yards and lay flat on the ground.

'What's she doing?' I whispered to her brother.

'Keep watching,' he replied.

'I want to see,' demanded Lucy. I took her up in my arms.

Some of the cows sat in the sunshine, while others munched grass. A pair of them watched Eilis. I bet they were thinking, *Hey, what's that crazy girl up to this time?* Some of the others soon turned their heads. Finally, one took a step forward. Then a second step. Others began to budge. Slowly they edged towards Eilis, becoming bolder as they got nearer till they stood in a semicircle around her, their noses tilted forwards, tails swishing.

I was amazed. 'What do you think of that?' I whispered in Lucy's ear. Her eyes were almost popping out of her head.

Eilis sat up. She spoke quietly to the cows, addressing them by name, telling them they were the best cows in the whole of Kerry. Then she got to her feet, saying, 'Well, girls, I'll say goodbye now.'

Sean elbowed me in the ribs. 'Did you hear the one about the cow who gave no milk?'

'Go on, tell me,' I said.

'She was an udder failure.'

I smiled.

'Want to hear another one?'

'Are you having to listen to Sean's terrible jokes?' said Eilis, climbing back over the gate.

'I've hundreds more,' said her brother.

'And they're pure torture,' added his sister.

'Were you not afraid of being trampled out there?' I asked.

'Never. They're pets, all of them,' she said.

Her older brother was in a nearby field harvesting potatoes. He put away his spade and came over. He smiled and said he would not shake our hands as his were too dirty, and then he asked a stream of questions. How did we like Kerry? Were we staying long? Was it sunnier than this in America? Would Lucy like to help dig some potatoes? He promised her a bag of them to bring home with her if she did. His name was Mike. He was eighteen.

'And we've a brother training to be a guard in Tipperary,' Eilis told me as we strolled on down the bohereen that cut through the farm. 'And another sister in Cork.'

'She's a nurse,' added Sean. 'Can we play *Mission: Impossible* now?'

But we had just spotted Mr Baker. He was sharpening a long curved blade with what looked like a smooth stone. If you've ever seen a picture of the Grim Reaper, you'll have noticed that he holds a big cutting instrument, called a scythe. Pat, Eilis's dad, had just used one to cut the grass along the length of the big field.

'You're definitely a Sullivan,' he said quietly as he squeezed – and I mean squeezed – my hand. He was a handsome dark-haired man who seemed a bit shy. He bent down to Lucy. 'And this little one is an O'Shea like her mother.' He held out his massive hand to my sister but she shrunk back and grabbed hold of me. I think the sight of the scythe must have freaked her out.

He showed me how to cut with it. The long wooden handle of the scythe had two hand-grips; he took hold of these and swung the blade underneath the grass, making sure to cut as close as possible to the ground. I stood back as Mr. Baker slowly but effortlessly swung his blade and the grass fell at his feet. Each swing of the scythe, each stroke of the blade mirrored the one that went before it and the one that came after it. I was impressed.

'Please can we play *Mission: Impossible?*' begged Sean.

'Okay,' I agreed.

'Let's start in the garden,' said Sean.

We split up into two teams. Me and Sean were the Impossible Missions Force team. Eilis and Lucy were the kidnappers. Well, kitten-nappers to be exact. The Bakers had a cat called Queenie and two kittens, whose names were Tipperty and Pip. We picked Tipperty, who up to then had been dozing happily under a bush by the front door.

'You have to give us a few minutes to get away,' said Eilis, taking up the little ball of fur.

'You can hide while we're getting our weapons,' said Sean.

'There's just one thing,' Eilis said to me. 'See that field over there?' She pointed to the one next to the potato field. 'Stay away from it – there's a bull there. And he's not very friendly.'

'Why do you have a bull?' I wanted to know.

Smiling at the question, she turned to her brother. 'What are we doing with the bull, Sean?'

Sean shrugged his shoulders and laughed.

'I was just wondering,' I said, beginning to feel foolish.

'Sure someone has to keep a bull, don't they?' said Eilis, giggling. 'Easy knowing you're a city boy!' She took my sister by the hand. 'Come on, Lucy, let's make ourselves scarce.' With that, they ran off.

I shook my head, thinking, *You walked into that one, didn't you, Danny.*

Sean had disappeared too – into the shed to procure some weapons. He quickly popped back out and handed me a hammer. 'That's your semi-automatic.'

'What's yours?' I said, staring at the tyre iron he was brandishing.

'A .45 Magnum.'

'Cool, let's get down to business,' I said.

We searched the outhouses first. Clasping his Magnum with both hands close to his chest, Agent Baker sidled towards the open doorway. I took one side; he took the other. At a nod from me, he sprang in, diving low to cover his side. Sean was really good at this game!

We cleared the outhouses but did not encounter our targets.

'Let's check the bohereen,' I ordered.

The bohereen was thick with vegetation and held dozens of hiding places. We flitted along silently, listening out for the slightest rustle in the undergrowth or a sign of movement. The bohereen split into a V, so I took the left side and Sean the right.

I began thinking about surfing and about getting to the beach today and about how it was time I phoned Jimmy, because he was surely back from Daytona Beach by now and would have loads of stuff on the Apollo launch. Suddenly, deep in these thoughts, I found myself staring through the gate at the bull.

He was dark-brown, massive and muscular, with stubby horns sticking out of his head. The steel ring through his snout didn't help his appearance either. I stood still, watching warily. Head down, he was eating the grass, though he seemed aware of me. With a quick jerk he lifted his head and stared me in the eye. His eyes were small, mean and glinting with menace. He snorted and came at me. For an instant I thought he might smash right through the gate. In fact, he whacked right into it – with his head, can you believe it? – and rattled it hard.

I nearly jumped out of my skin.

Just then I heard the girls' voices calling from somewhere up around the house. They were teasing us. 'Come and get us! Come and get us!'

I ran back and met Agent Baker. We hotfooted it towards our targets. When we came to the yard, we slowed and crept forward, communicating only by hand signals. He took one side of the house; I took the other.

One thing – correction, two things – my little sister can't do when she's excited is stay still and keep quiet. In the yard, there was a big shrub covered in blue blossoms and it was moving. I could hear my sister giggling.

I pounced with a mighty roar. 'This is the I.M.F.! Hands up!'

My sister screeched and froze, but Eilis sprang like a gazelle. With one bound, she was away. Tiny Tipperty went scurrying off in the opposite direction.

Sean came racing round the corner of the house. 'Bang! Bang!' he yelled, confronting her with his .45 Magnum. 'Gotcha!'

'Missed!' Eilis cried, trying to veer past him. But Sean grabbed her by the arm and dived on top of her. The pair of them went tumbling to the ground, laughing. I joined in the fun and next thing my little sister raced over and dived in too. We all laughed our heads off.

Then I heard Mom calling us. It was time to leave.

'Will you be going to the creamery tomorrow?' I asked Eilis.

'Eight o'clock in the morning,' said Eilis. 'Like to come?'

12

Apollo is a good name for the space programme. If you're shooting for the stars it's best to have the god of light and of archery on your side. My mom probably knows more about Apollo the god than she does about Apollo the space rocket. Being a painter, I guess she sees things differently.

Apollo was also the Greek god of healing, according to Mom. She painted four pictures of him earlier this year and sold them all except one, which she kept for me. It's hanging on my bedroom wall. It shows a fellow about my age but with long golden hair (mine's brown) flying out of the dark void of space on a wave of colour and light. When you look at it, he's coming right at you, like a surfer on the crest of cascading rainbow colours.

Mom gave it to me on my birthday. She gave me a tight hug and said: 'I hope you like it. It could be you, Danny.'

Aunt Mary, who knows lots about painting, came up to my room to see it. 'Your mom's an expressionist,' she whispered after gazing at Apollo.

'What's that?' I wanted to know.

'Someone who knows how to express feeling in a painting,' she said.

I liked the painting, but I didn't get this 'expressionist' stuff.

Apollo would have been a cool surfer, though.

Mom drove to the beach that afternoon with my plank sticking out the rear window. I couldn't wait to use it.

The sight of that beach, with those long, smooth waves glinting in the sun, brought a smile to my face. It was almost deserted, and I was secretly glad because when you're learning to surf you don't want lots of people staring at you.

I left my board on the sand and walked to the water's edge. There was only one way to get down in this freezing water. I counted to three. Then, with a roar I charged. I flung out my arms and dived headlong into the incoming wave. The shock of hitting that water was something else. But at least I was down.

I carried the board into the water and lay flat on it. It was a relief to see that it supported my weight. Then I tried paddling, and that worked well too. Mom waved from the shore and I waved back. I wanted to show her what I could do.

Maybe I'll belly-board first, just to see how it goes, I thought. All you do is lie flat on the board, hold on and ride in with the wave … It should be easy, I know. But when the first wave came it toppled me right off the board. So did the second one.

That was enough of belly-boarding. I decided to skip to the next level.

One of the many good things about this beach was that the waves were regular and well spaced. You could see what was coming and you'd time to prepare for it. I got back up on the board, paddled into position and waited for the right one. I was quite a while waiting for it. In fact, I was blue with the cold and about to give up when the right one finally arrived.

Looking over my shoulder I saw it gliding towards me, nothing too big or spectacular, just a four-foot wave running to shore. I started paddling like crazy, trying to get enough speed to hook up with it. Suddenly I felt the board lift as the wave caught up with me. I sprang up. That wave must have had my name on it because I stayed up.

With the nose of my plank arrowing out of the wave and the water foaming around my feet, I flew through the air – like Apollo himself. But just for a second. All too quickly, the wave collapsed into an explosion of foam and I was sent flying.

Despite many more efforts, I failed to catch another wave before the cold drove me from the water.

Later that evening, we went to visit Mom's cousin who lives at the foot of the big mountain across the bay. Mom said the mountain was called Mount Brandon and was the second tallest mountain in the country. 'It's named after a holy man called Brendan,' she told us as we drove towards it. 'He discovered America long before Columbus did.'

'Says who?' I smiled.

'Says me and everyone in Ireland,' said Mom, glancing at me in the rear-view mirror.

'You don't really believe it, do you?' I responded.

'I do. I'm serious,' she replied.

'Yeah, but you believe in fairies and leprechauns as well, Mom!'

'I believe in fairies too, Mommy,' piped up Lucy.

'Good girl, I know you do, and so does your grandfather,' said Mom.

Mom's cousin, Maureen, lived with her husband and four kids in a house much like my grandpa's, though not quite as bare. They had no TV either. We sat around a turf fire chatting and eating more scones and jam. Maureen's husband sang some songs in Irish. His name was Danny, too, and Mom said he was famous for his singing.

It was late when we headed home.

Lucy was fast asleep in the back of the car. I sat in the front with Mom, watching the moths flitting into our headlights as we wound along the narrow, pitch-dark country lane.

I must have nodded off briefly when I felt Mom nudging my arm.

'Look, Danny,' she whispered.

We were stopped on Grandpa's bohereen, the engine ticking over quietly.

I sat up and peered out. The fox stood stone-still in the glare of our lights, about fifteen yards ahead, her eyes shining like two silver discs. She was smaller than I had imagined but she looked scary, like a visitor from another world standing there unafraid, watching us, the light mountain mist drifting around her.

Then, like a phantom, she disappeared.

13

A crashing sound of cartwheels split the morning air. Long before her horse came round the bend, I knew it was Eilis.

I was sitting up on the ditch waiting for her. Only a few minutes earlier I had woken with a start. I had dressed in a hurry, snatched an apple from the kitchen and cut down through the field to the road.

Two farmers had passed by on their carts. My watch said 7.55. Had I missed her? I sat in the sunshine, munching my apple, gazing at Mount Brandon.

Once more she came thundering around the bend, up on her feet like a charioteer. This was going to be another white-knuckle ride. I took a last bite of my apple and jumped onto the road.

Given the speed of the horse, it was impressive the way she brought it to a halt. Her brown eyes smiled down at me.

'Where do I sit?' I enquired.

'Right there.' She tapped the front corner of the cart with her foot. 'You can put your legs over the side. Hold tight now.'

I hadn't even taken up my position when she let out a low whistle and the horse sprang into action. To say he took off like a jet engine would be a slight exaggeration, but it felt that way. We stormed down the road, making enough noise to 'waken the dead', as Mom would say.

Surfing had nothing on this! I was perched on the side of the cart like some seasick trapeze artist, my hands clutching the edge of the boards, my legs dangling right next to that great spinning wheel.

Why did I let myself in for this? I thought.

I broke into a cold sweat as we approached the first bend. Instead of slowing, the horse speeded up. She gave him free rein and made a clicking noise with her tongue and he swished his tail like crazy. One was as bad – or mad – as the other.

As we swung around the bend warm milk slopped out of the churn onto my neck. I thought of astronauts. Was that what riding a g-force felt like, a mad pulling sensation that leaves you sick and exhilarated at the same time?

Immediately we swerved into another bend. We came out of that one too. I glanced up at Eilis. She had this look of one hundred per cent focus, command and confidence. I started to breathe again. If – and I admit it's a big if – you ever wanted someone to take you on a cart ride at 100 mph down a narrow, winding country road, then Eilis Baker was the one to ask.

We flew down a straight stretch of road before meeting more twists and turns. I lost my balance on one of these and almost fell off the cart. Then, as we came to the final deadly bend, we caught up with the two farmers who had passed earlier. One was directly behind the other. I wondered would Eilis fly past. Lucky for me, she reined in the horse and fell in behind them.

She looked at me and grinned. 'Good road manners are important.'

'No comment,' I said.

It must have been rush hour because there was a line of carts at the creamery. There were old men with their worn jackets and caps, and young guys in shirtsleeves – some with horses, some with donkeys, others with tractors. Everyone stood chatting in the warm sunshine.

With my T-shirt, jeans and sneakers, I felt like I was sticking out a mile. My mom had told me that an American is known as a Yank over here, but not to be upset because it was a friendly expression.

One of the men approached the cart. He shook my hand and introduced himself.

'I knew your father,' he told me in a quiet voice. 'I was very sorry when I heard the sad news.'

'Thank you, sir,' I mumbled.

Another man came over and said the same thing. He told me he had often played football with my dad and said how much I looked like him. It was kind of awkward and gave me a strange feeling in my stomach.

In the end our turn came. Eilis steered her horse alongside the creamery wall to the platform where two men stood waiting. They reached down together, picked up one of the churns and poured the milk into a big vat to weigh it.

I expected Eilis to race home straight away. Instead she sat down and took it easy.

'Everyone remembers your dad,' she said.

'I know,' I said, deciding to change the subject. 'Eilis, I heard some people are making a movie round here.'

'Yes. It's called *Ryan's Daughter*. They've been making it for months and months and even built a whole village for it on the back of the mountain there.'

'Have you seen Robert Mitchum?' I asked.

'No, but he was in the village one day buying a newspaper. He's a character, they say.'

'I have to see this movie set,' I said.

'I'll bring you some day so.'

'Cool,' I said.

She dropped me off at Grandpa's bohereen. We said we'd meet up later at her farm.

Grandpa and his dog were in the yard when I got back. The dog was lying on the grass, panting gently in the heat. I noticed the ladder was still propped up against the wall.

'You survived the trip to the creamery,' he remarked.

'But will you survive going up on that roof again?' I replied.

'I've a spot of painting to do, that's all,' he said. He looked at me with that mischievous twinkle in his eye. 'Tell me, in America, do they really believe a rocket is going to the moon? With men inside it?'

I could see Grandpa wasn't going to let go of this one. 'That's what they believe, sir.'

He threw his eyes up to heaven. 'In all seriousness!'

'You're the one who can't be serious,' I replied.

'Let me tell you a story, a true story,' he began. 'One morning a long time ago – I don't remember the exact year: it was back in the twenties – my mother was out here in the garden, standing where we are now, hanging out the clothes to dry, when she heard an unusual noise coming from somewhere. I was inside the house at the time. Suddenly I heard her calling, "Quick, John! Come out!" So out I ran, and there she was waving her hands in the air. I looked up and saw an airplane, a small airplane, passing over the fields. It was flying low and you could see the man inside it. And he was waving back to us. Of course we had never seen the likes of an airplane before. I was amazed! Then it turned away and flew off over the side of the mountain there.' He paused. 'Do you know who it was?'

I shook my head.

'That was the man himself, Charles Lindbergh.'

I gasped. '*The* Charles Lindbergh? In the *Spirit of St Louis*?'

'Aye, that was the name of the plane.'

'Then the year was 1927,' I said. 'The first transatlantic flight.'

'He flew all the way from America and I saw it here with my own two eyes.'

'Wow, that is something!'

'But who'll get to see them flying to the moon? No-one will. That's my point.'

'It'll be on TV.'

'TV!' he scoffed. 'That's just trickery.'

'Hundreds of thousands of people will go to Cape Kennedy to watch the lift off,' I told him.

'No-one will see a lift off. It's all a big hoax,' he insisted.

'No, it's not,' I shouted. 'I saw John Glenn shoot into orbit – with my own two eyes! My dad brought me.'

'Is that so?' he said.

I told him the story of that day and I think it made some impression. But folks will believe what folks want to believe. Anyway, we left it at that. He went to his ladder; I went inside for breakfast.

Mom and Lucy were at the kitchen table. Lucy, in pyjamas, was nibbling toast. Mom was writing a list. 'Danny, we're going to go to Tralee one day to get some things for your grandfather,' she announced. 'Like a refrigerator.'

'He doesn't need a refrigerator,' I said. The way I saw it, Grandpa was a cowboy. Do cowboys need refrigerators? Did the Magnificent Seven have refrigerators?

'And I want to get him a phone.'

'I don't see him wanting one of those either,' I said.

'He does too, Danny!' cut in my little sister.

'Maybe not,' said Mom, 'but at least we'll be able to call *him*.'

'Yeah, we'll call Grandpa!' cried Lucy. 'I love Grandpa!'

'Okay, point taken,' I said.

Later that afternoon I went down to the Bakers' place. Lucy insisted on coming with me.

Straight away she wanted to see the bull, which had been moved to the field next to the farmhouse. She picked up some hay, climbed up on the gate and started calling the bull softly: 'Here, Moo-moo! Come here, Moo-moo!'

I pointed out to her that this was a daddy cow, not a mommy cow. 'And he's really mean and dangerous,' I added.

'He's not mean, Danny,' she threw back at me.

'He is too,' I said, taking her by the hand and leading her away.

Eilis and Mike were in the field opposite, turning the cut hay with pitchforks to let the sun dry it out. I picked up a pitchfork and helped while Lucy and Sean played hide-and-seek nearby. The field stretched down towards the sea and there was a lot of hay to turn. The sun beat down on my shoulders and soon I was sweating.

Eilis was trying to keep up with her big brother and I was trying to be as fast as Eilis. I guess you could call it a three-way race. I didn't want to be beaten by a girl. But she was used to this kind of work. We turned one row of hay after another with no let-up. I found myself falling behind. My hands grew sore; my arms ached.

Hey, I'm supposed to be on vacation here, I thought. *This is too much like hard work.*

Finally, after an hour, at the end of another row, I stuck my pitchfork into the ground. 'I need some water,' I said.

'Well and good.' Eilis slammed her pitchfork into the earth. 'Let's go.'

The Bakers' spring was just a hole in the ground but the water was cool and clean. We got down on our knees, cupped our hands and drank our fill. I splashed myself to cool down. Then we all splashed each other like crazy people.

The spring was close to the boundary with my grandfather's farm. I pointed to the big outcrop of rock that I had spotted across the next field. 'You reckon that's where the fox hangs out?' I asked.

'You can be sure,' Eilis replied.

'Can we take a look?' I said. To my mind, searching for foxes beats turning hay any day.

'Lead the way,' said Eilis. Turning to Sean and Lucy, she put a finger to her lips. 'You two will be as quiet as mice, won't you?'

The pair of them nodded. It seems my sister can be quiet when she wants to be.

Instead of making a bee-line for the rocks, we circled the field under cover of the ditch. On the far side we met a bohereen that brought us quite close to the outcrop. I wanted to get nearer, though.

'We need to get down and crawl,' I whispered over my shoulder. I pointed to a large boulder a short distance from the main outcrop.

'Danny, do foxes bite?' my sister whispered.

I turned and saw her little face full of worry. 'Of course not,' I said.

'I want to go home.'

'You can't. Follow me.'

'No … I'm scared.'

It's funny, she had no fear of a bull, yet a fox scared her.

Eilis took her by the hand. 'Come with me, girl. I'll mind you.'

Sean and I crawled ahead like commandos to the cover of the rock. I stuck my head out and took a look. Two foxes were lying out in the sunshine as if waiting for us. They were cubs, just a few months old. Suddenly another one appeared. This fellow was frisky and full of energy. He sprang up to the other pair and started pouncing around them. In an instant the three of them were chasing, dodging and grappling with each other.

Lucy cowered behind the rock, afraid to take a look. I reached back and picked her up. I felt her little fingers digging into my arms. But when I stood up with her the cubs must have spotted us. In the blink of an eye, they were gone.

We strolled back across the fields.

'I'd advise you not to tell your grandfather about them – or there'll be war,' Eilis warned us.

'Do you hear that, Lucy?' I said. 'We don't tell Grandpa about the foxes. It's a secret, okay?'

14

I needed to talk to Jimmy to find out what was going on back home. This vacation was fun but I would miss the space launch because of it. In a few days *Apollo 11* would blast off for the moon. In Florida the atmosphere would be electric ... If Dad were around, we'd be going to the launch for sure.

I remembered the *Apollo 8* mission last Christmas. Who could ever forget it? The launch had been perfect. One after another the three stages of the Saturn V rocket ignited, sending astronauts Frank Borman, Jim Lovell and Bill Anders into orbit. This time, they didn't jettison the third stage. They relit it instead and rocketed out of earth's orbit and into space. No humans had dared venture beyond earth's orbit before. But the *Apollo 8* crew aimed to fly right up to and around the moon and back again!

They looked out their window and saw planet earth drifting away from them.

Twelve hours into the mission, they were 70,000 miles out and earth was the size of a baseball.

At 140,000 miles out they held a live telecast. I could hardly believe my eyes as I watched the three weightless astronauts floating around in space. One of the guys – I think it was Anders – started brushing his teeth. He let go of the brush and it began twirling in the air, in slow motion, right in front of him. Then he reached out and took it back.

At 200,000 miles, the earth was the size of a marble, the astronauts told us, a beautiful blue marble.

Finally, after three days, the three men approached the moon and prepared to slot into its orbit. Yet they still couldn't see it. However, as they slipped in behind it, they would know it was there because the moon would block radio contact with earth.

And so they disappeared behind the moon and the radio fell silent. The world waited to hear from them.

Right on cue, they reappeared, swinging around the corner of the moon's near side at an altitude of just 69 miles.

The guy in Mission Control welcomed them back. 'What does the moon look like?' he wanted to know, like the rest of us.

'It's got no colour,' came the answer. 'Like a beach.'

They flew on, over the lonely and desolate moonscape, pointing out the Sea of Crises, the Sea of Fertility and the Marsh of Sleep. One of them described it as a 'great expanse of nothing'.

The moon wasn't exactly a friendly place.

Christmas hadn't been much fun in our house in recent years. But that 24 December 1968 was special. With the lights on our Christmas tree twinkling like stars, me and Mom, with Lucy cradled in her arms, sat glued to our TV. Everyone had been saying what a horrible year it had been. Martin Luther King had been murdered. They had killed Robert Kennedy too. In Vietnam, in faraway Asia, a war was raging out of control and young American soldiers were dying. Here at home there were riots in the streets. It seemed the world was a mess. Yet, as the three astronauts circled the barren desert of the moon and saw the far-off earth rise above it, they showed us what our earth really was: a beautiful jewel shining in a dark universe.

They ended the telecast with a reading: 'In the beginning God created the Heavens and the earth ...' Each astronaut took turns to read. Then, Frank Borman finished with the words: 'And God called the dry land earth, and the gathering of the waters he called seas. And God saw that it was good.'

Then he signed off. 'Good luck, Merry Christmas and God bless all of you on the good earth.'

At that moment, Mom took my hand and squeezed it. 'The earth *is* good, Danny,' she said, then she smiled. I hadn't seen her smile like that for a long time.

15

I slept it out the next morning and missed the ride to the creamery.

Over breakfast, I planned out my day. First, I'd call over to Eilis's place for a while. After that, I'd go surfing. Later in the afternoon, I'd visit the post office, the only place around here where I could phone Jimmy.

I'd call him around 4 p.m., which would be 10 a.m. back home. I counted out the money I needed. The Irish money was so big and heavy compared to ours. All the coins had animals stamped on them: chickens, rabbits, pigs, horses and so on. The pictures were pretty but the coins were way too large.

Mrs Baker opened the door to me, as friendly as ever.

'Hello young fella. Eilis and Sean are upstairs with the grasshoppers,' she told me, throwing her eyes to heaven. 'It's like a zoo up there. Go on up to them.'

I climbed the steep stairs, curious about the grasshopper bit. One of the bedroom doors had a handwritten sign on it: *The Greenlee Library.* I knocked twice and entered.

Eilis and her brother were stretched out on the floor before a big glass jar. They seemed surprised to see me. 'So it's yourself,' she said with a smile.

'Do you want to see the grasshopper Olympics?' asked Sean.

The 'Greenlee Library' had a large bookcase crammed with books. The walls were covered with pictures and drawings of animals, mainly horses, with a few dolphins and mice thrown in for good measure. 'Is your horse called Lir?' I asked, noticing the name on the pencil drawings.

'That's the name,' she replied. 'Would you like a ride on him?'

'Sure,' I said. 'But I've never been up on a horse before.'

'I'll show you,' she said.

'Cool.'

Sean banged the jar with a pen. 'Jump, will you? Jump!' he exhorted the grasshoppers.

'What's that?' I asked, pointing to a tiny polished skull on the shelf.

'That was a rabbit,' she replied. 'I found it on the beach.'

Eilis was what you call a collector. On the shelf, on the study table and on the window ledge, I saw pretty pebbles in a brass box, feathers of various birds, some glistening white rocks, sea-shells, a large rusted key, a small and beautiful green bottle, a tiny bird's nest, three painted eggshells (duck eggs, Eilis informed me, and she had painted them herself) and – loveliest of all – a glass fishing float, the colour of ocean blue.

'I like your room,' I said.

As I crouched down by the great grasshopper jar, I noticed a similar jar behind the bed, with the same layer of grass and leaves inside. 'What have you got in there?' I asked.

'Caterpillars,' she replied cheerfully.

I peered into the jar and saw the little green and yellow guys busily nibbling away. A small stick was positioned against the inside of the jar.

'The lollipop stick is for them to hang off when they change into a chrysalis,' said Eilis.

'Hop, will ye!' cried Sean, turning again on the grasshoppers.

'Come on, we'll let them go,' his sister suddenly decided.

We trooped down the stairs, out into the yard and released some mightily relieved grasshoppers into the long grass.

'Do you want to ride the horse now?' Eilis suggested.

'Sure,' I said.

Lir was in the big field with the cattle. Eilis brought out a bridle and called to him. He immediately came – walking, not galloping, to my relief.

Relax, Danny, this is going to be okay, I thought to myself.

Lir stood obediently as Eilis slipped on the bridle.

'There's no saddle, right?' I enquired.

'Just bareback,' said Eilis. She turned to me and smiled. 'Are you ready?'

'You bet,' I said, trying to pep myself up.

'Here, I'll give you a boost,' she said, bending down to link her hands.

'That's okay, I can do it myself,' I told her.

I made two attempts to mount that horse. In the first, I tried to grip the back of his neck and spring on board, like they do in the movies. This failed, mainly because I chickened out of grabbing him by the mane – who knows how he might have responded? Then I tried the run-and-jump-onto-his-back technique. That bombed as well.

'Come here, boy.' Eilis beckoned to me and linked her hands again.

I needed the help and so I took it. But when I sat up on Lir and shook the reins, he wouldn't move.

'Giddy-up, fella,' I said.

Nothing.

I clicked my tongue and shook the reins.

Nothing.

I clicked again, shook the reins again and dug my heels into his sides.

Do you think that horse would move?

I heard Eilis's voice behind me. 'Come on, Lir.'

Suddenly, she whacked the horse on the backside and all hell broke loose.

Lir shot away like a stone from a sling. It was over in an instant. I mustn't have had a proper grip on those reins because I fell right smack onto the ground.

Sean laughed hysterically.

I was momentarily stunned. Then I saw that I had fallen right into a cowpat – a fresh cowpat. Man, it was all over me, my shirt and jeans.

Eilis turned away from me, her hand over her mouth, her shoulders shaking.

I saw red.

'It's not funny,' I said coldly. I ran my fingers through my hair and noticed that it had gotten into my hair too – from my hands.

At this, Sean collapsed into hysterics. Eilis could no longer contain herself and was laughing loudly too with her legs crossed.

'It's *not funny!*' I exploded.

This brought the house down, making them laugh even more.

I stormed off.

I was in a rage all the way back to Grandpa's. *Who do they think they are? How can they laugh like that? It's not funny. I wouldn't laugh if it happened to one of them*, I fumed. *Look at me, I'm covered in it! How am I going to get it off? And my grandpa doesn't even have a shower…*

Of course, Mom and Lucy seemed to find it funny as well. I was glad my grandfather wasn't around because he'd have laughed too.

Anyway, after a wash, a change of clothes and some lunch, I felt a lot better. Lucy sat in my lap and I read her a few stories.

Mom says I'm like my dad in lots of ways. He was easygoing, and so am I. It was hard to get him angry, she says, but if you got him angry then it was like a volcano erupting. But it always blew over quickly, she says. And it's like that with me too – well, most of the time.

I decided to stick with my game-plan for the day.

After lunch, I borrowed my grandfather's bike and headed for the beach. If you're having a bad day, there's nothing like surfing to sort you out. My board was where I'd left it, in a grassy hollow above the beach, so I got down to business right away.

A breeze was building up and the waves were bigger than I'd expected. I must have been lucky riding the board the way I did the other day, because today was quite different. Could I stand up on it? If I fell once, I fell ten times. But this time I didn't mind at all. It was fun splashing in the waves and getting dunked too. It helps being a good swimmer – thanks to my dad. He taught me when I was a toddler.

Then, on surely the eleventh try, I caught a wave for a few giddy and fantastic moments. It was like flying.

An hour had gone by before I got out. To warm up afterwards I ran the whole length of the beach.

Afterwards I cycled up to the village only to find the post office had shut for the day – for the weekend in fact. Jimmy would have to wait till Monday.

16

Mom was nervous, I could tell.

When I'm nervous, everything slows down and I have to think twice before doing anything or saying anything. When Mom's nervous, everything speeds up a little, the way she talks and what she does. She was like that now as we prepared to visit my dad's parents. She put a new dress on Lucy and tied ribbons in her hair. Mom even tied back her own hair, which is most unusual, and swapped her jeans for a skirt, something she rarely does. When I came down the stairs in a T-shirt and jeans, I was told to go back and put on a shirt and tie. I did as I was told to keep her happy. I guess I wanted to make a good impression too. Like my mom, I was nervous – perhaps more nervous for her than anything else, wondering how friendly they would be.

'Do you think we'll be back before ten?' I asked as we got ready to leave.

'Why do you ask?'

'Sean says there's some kind of barn dance on in the village tonight and everyone's going.' I had met Sean earlier on my way back from the beach. His sister wasn't around; she had gone shopping in the town with her mother.

Mom raised her eyebrows. 'A barn dance – is that the name you give it? I'll have you know it's called a *céilí*.' (kay-lee)

'Well?' I enquired.

'Well what?'

'The *céilí* – tonight?'

'You can forget about that, sonny.'

'Come on, Mom!'

She raised those eyebrows again, but her eyes were smiling. 'You must want to dance with Eilis, do you?'

I threw my eyes up to heaven.

'Don't worry. There'll be another one next Saturday,' she added, ushering us out the door.

We drove through the village and followed the road that skirted the pyramid mountain. Everyone was quiet, even Lucy. I guess she must have been feeling those nervous vibrations too.

'Guess what,' said Mom, breaking the silence, 'the most westerly point in Ireland is only a few miles up the road. After that, the next stop is America.'

A moment later, she pulled off into a side-road and stopped. 'Well, here we are,' she said.

'Are we in America?' asked Lucy.

'No, darling!' laughed Mom.

A stone's-throw away, I saw a farmhouse similar to Grandpa's. The sea was just a few hundred yards away. We had scarcely driven three miles. I was amazed my other grandparents' place had been so close to us, but I made no comment.

We got out of the auto. Mom brushed down her skirt and fixed her hair again. She looked tense.

We walked towards the house.

'Hey, Mom, you forgot the gifts,' I reminded her.

'Well remembered, Danny,' said Mom. She hurried back to the automobile and took out the two gifts, wrapped in fancy paper. She gave the big one to me – 'for your grandpa' – and the smaller one to Lucy – 'for Grandma'. She cleared her throat as we came up to the house.

We didn't have to knock. A small old lady with a kind face opened the door. Any worries I had about the meeting vanished.

She held out her arms to Mom and they embraced each other. She turned to Lucy then, cupped her hands around my sister's face and tearfully kissed her on the forehead. She did the same to me, all the time whispering something to us in Irish.

Inside, the house was like my grandpa's, except there was linoleum on the floor, pictures on the walls – including a framed photograph of President Kennedy – and lots of things, like jugs and little porcelain angels, on shelves. She brought out a photo of my dad.

'It's the only one we have of him,' she said. 'I used to have it up on the wall there, but I couldn't bear to look at it so I took it down.' Mom hugged her again then and the pair of them were sniffling and talking once more in Irish, looking at the picture, glancing at me.

'What are you saying?' I asked.

But of course I knew.

They handed me the black-and-white photo. It showed my dad sitting on a ladder resting against a large haystack. The sun was shining and he was smiling, looking down. He seemed about eighteen years old. Looking at him looking at me – and looking so like me – it felt like he was there, right there in the room.

But the thing is he wasn't. He was gone, wasn't he?

I handed the photo back to Grandma. And I was glad when my other grandfather came into the house that very minute. I was able to give him the gift, a huge sweater Mom had bought. Lucy, on cue, gave her gift, an expensive-looking teapot, to our grandma. There were more smiles then and then everyone relaxed. Tea was made – in the new teapot of course – and a tray of sandwiches and a homemade cake brought out. My dad's older brother, Uncle Tom, joined us. He had stayed back to run the family farm and, I guess, look after his parents (he wasn't married). There was another brother in Australia, a sister in England, a sister in the States and two other brothers who were teachers in Dublin. Up till now, I'd only met the sister in Chicago.

The grown-ups sat around drinking tea and talking. Soon Lucy grew restless. 'Are there chickens here?' she kept asking me out loud. Uncle Tom soon got the message and invited Lucy and me on a tour of the homestead. They didn't keep chickens but they had a donkey, he told us, and would Lucy like to take him for a ride? She nodded enthusiastically and pretty soon we were leading Pluto (the name Lucy gave the donkey) down the road with my sister perched on his back.

The evening breeze had strengthened into a strong wind, blowing in from the sea. Hearing the deep boom of breaking waves, I asked, 'Is there a beach down here?'

He nodded. 'It's where your father used to swim. He was the only swimmer among us – he taught himself.'

The road descended sharply and I found myself gazing at a craggy cove overlooked by cliffs. My attention quickly turned to the huge breakers charging into it. 'My dad swam in that?' I gasped.

The heaving sea resembled a battlefield, over which plumes of spray drifted. Through the narrow mouth of the cove the smoking breakers came in like the US 2nd Armoured Division in an unstoppable advance. On either side, waves smacked into the sheer wall with detonations of spray that pelted over the top of the cliff itself. Meanwhile, the main column of water surged through the middle, swelling massively as it drew near till it suddenly reared up and broke with hellish fury.

'He swam in that?' I repeated.

'Even in seas like that,' said Tom. 'He was a powerful swimmer, your father.'

The beach was only about three hundred yards in length. Great strands of kelp and the remains of crabs were scattered along the shore. A massive tree trunk had been tossed up and left high and dry on the sand. We walked to the far corner where, sheltered by the cliff, it was quieter. Uncle Tom pointed to where the rock hung in great smooth yellow slabs. 'See that writing on the rock up there? Your father left that. Climb up and take a look.'

I could make out something carved in the rock, quite high up, above a ledge.

After scaling the rock – it was not difficult to do – I saw in neat chiselled letters the words:

JOHN SULLIVAN MAY 1952

'What do you think of that then?' Uncle Tom called up.

I had a lump in my throat but I pulled myself together. 'That must have taken a long time to do,' I said.

'Aye, shortly before he left for America,' said my uncle.

It was late when we drove back through the village. The lights were on in the hall, the windows were open and you could hear the music in the air.

'There'll be another *céilí* next Saturday,' said Mom.

I said nothing because right then I didn't care. I didn't feel like dancing.

17

It was a Monday in November, in Chicago.

The moment I woke up, on that morning four years ago, I knew something was wrong.

I never wake up for school: I have to be called by Mom, and it's still like that today. That morning, though, my mom never came to my room. I lay there a while until I heard Lucy squawking. So I got out of bed. But before I could get to her I saw Mom standing outside her door, looking pale and distracted, as if she didn't know what to do. Then she lowered her head and pressed a clenched fist against her forehead. That was when she saw me.

'What's up?' I said.

'Oh, Danny, nothing. Everything's going to be all right.' She sighed as if in pain. She held out her hands to me (she'd Lucy's bottle in one of them). As she hugged me tight, she groaned and cried out, 'I keep telling them it's all a mistake!'

'Who?' I said.

'Aunt Joan and Luke. They're downstairs …' she answered, her voice trailing away. By now Lucy was brewing up a storm. Mom let go of me and went to her.

I don't like the sound of this, I thought and went back to my room and dressed. It never entered my mind that this might have something to do with Dad.

I walked downstairs. The clock on the wall said 8.35. *I am way late for school*, I thought.

Aunt Joan, my dad's sister, and her husband, Luke, were sitting on the sofa. Luke is a police officer, like my dad, but he wasn't in uniform. He stood up when I entered. Aunt Joan was clutching a tissue. She was trembling, I noticed.

'What's up?' I shrugged.

Luke looked at me as if he didn't know what to say. He turned to Aunt Joan, who just sat huddled on the sofa staring straight ahead.

'Is everything all right?' I asked.

'It's about your father, Danny.' Luke is a big guy from Colorado, built like a heavyweight boxer, but even his voice sounded weak and hoarse. 'There's been a crash, and it doesn't look good, buddy.'

Then my aunt stood up and came over and hugged me like she would never let me go. 'I'm so sorry, Danny … I'm so sorry.'

I pulled away from her. 'What's going on?'

Mom came in with Lucy in her arms. My sister, who was only a few months old, was quiet now, happily guzzling her bottle. 'Joan and Luke think something's happened to your dad, but I keep telling them it's all right, it's just a mistake, it's going to be all right,' said Mom. She was even smiling now; she really meant what she was saying. 'He'll be back shortly. Believe me, he'll walk right in that door and when he does, boy, he's going to have some explaining to do!'

Aunt Joan followed her into the kitchen and I could hear her talking to Mom in a low voice.

I didn't know what to think or do. I looked at Luke.

'I got a call this morning, Danny. Four a.m.. From one of the guys. He told me your dad had been in a crash and it looked bad. So … So I've been to the hospital and it is bad, I'm afraid. John didn't make it.'

'What happened?'

'There was some ... he skidded off the road.'

It was past midday before they persuaded Mom to go down to the hospital. She still believed it was all a horrible mistake and told me not to worry. Luke drove her down and Aunt Joan stayed with me and Lucy.

Soon people were calling at our apartment – friends and police officers who worked with Dad. Mrs Warner, the old lady on the next floor, arrived with sandwiches and a plate of homemade cookies especially for me. I ate them too, every one.

And when Mom arrived back from hospital, she still had not accepted anything was wrong and kept saying it wasn't him. She grew upset. 'Why won't anyone believe me?' she cried out. 'What's up with you all?' Aunt Joan and Mrs Warner had to keep their arms around her the whole time because it looked like she might faint, but still she wouldn't sit down and kept on talking about Dad coming home until Aunt Joan took her into the bedroom to try and get her to lie down for a while. But that didn't work either.

A lot of that day, and the days that came after it, are hazy in my memory. I don't care to remember them much anyway.

Mom's sister, Aunt Mary, flew up from Florida and stayed on with us for a week after the funeral. But when she returned home, we were pretty much on our own. Except for Mrs Warner, that is. Every day she brought me to school, because Mom wasn't really up to it. And she collected me too. She was a small, round woman with sore knees, but that didn't stop her going up and down the stairs to us. She came by with meals most days or cooked dinners for us in our apartment. Mrs Warner sort of took us – Mom, Lucy, me – under her wing. She had lost her own husband only two years back, she said. She said he was a wonderful man as well, like my dad. She had two children, she told us, who were grown up and had kids of their own. But she didn't get to see her grandchildren much because they lived out of state.

But even with Mrs Warner's help things were pretty rough. Mom didn't have much to say any more, and Lucy seemed to cry all the time. We never went out, not even to the park. Our apartment looked like a bomb site and it felt like a tomb.

Then, a month or two later, early in the New Year, Aunt Mary came to visit again. She told Mom she wanted us to move to Florida and stay with her for a while.

So we moved to Sarasota and lived in a house with palm trees in the garden by the sea. It's where Mom began to paint and Lucy began to walk.

And me? I don't know. I couldn't say, really.

18

Lucy wanted to visit the Bakers so that gave me an excuse, as I felt a bit stupid about the horse episode. Sean greeted us in the yard, as he struggled to carry a big bucket of water.

'How was the *céilí*?' I enquired.

'Great altogether. Pity you missed it,' he replied.

Eilis came out of the house. She smiled at Lucy and me, and I smiled back.

'I'm sorry about yesterday,' I said. 'I didn't mean–'

'Forget about yesterday, boy,' she cut in. 'Anyway, we shouldn't have laughed at you.'

Her brother pointed his finger at her. 'And she's smiling today because she's got a new boyfriend.'

'Oh yeah?' I said.

'Don't mind him,' said Eilis.

'She met him at the *céilí*!' Sean sang out.

'Stop that, you,' said his sister.

'A Jackeen from Dublin!'

'What's a Jackeen?' I wanted to know.

'Ask Eily, she knows,' laughed Sean.

'I'll take a switch to you if you're not careful,' his sister threatened.

'And what's a switch?' I asked.

'I'll show you,' cried Eilis and she ran to the ditch and pulled a big yellow weed and went racing after her brother, trying to hit him on the legs.

He then grabbed a switch of his own and went after her. 'Go

on, Sean,' I encouraged him from the sidelines. Whereupon Eilis stopped and looked at me. Then she turned to Sean. 'I've a better idea,' she told him. 'Let's get the boy from America!'

'Why not?' her brother agreed.

Next thing both of them came at me with their switches. But I got hold of the bucket of water and turned the game around. I chased them, and when the bucket was empty they chased me. It was only then that I noticed Lucy wasn't around. 'Where's she gone to?' I asked the others.

We called her a couple of times and looked in the barn. The cats were curled up in the straw, but there was no sign of her. I shouted out her name again. Sean went to look in the garden; Eilis headed down the bohereen.

Then I had a hunch. I walked around the side of the barn and, sure enough, found my sister standing up on the gate, clutching a tiny fistful of grass for the bull.

'Lucy, I told you not to go there,' I scolded as I hauled her off the gate. 'And you must have heard me calling you.'

'I want to see Daddy Moo-moo,' she answered.

'I told you to stay away from him,' I said.

'He's lonely,' she protested.

'He's not lonely. He's a bull,' I said. I picked her up. 'Come on,' I said, 'I'll show you some real moo-cows.'

'He is lonely too. He's all on his own.'

'No, he's not. He wants to be alone because he doesn't like people.'

'He likes me, he does!' she said indignantly.

Eilis arrived back and saw Lucy pouting. She stroked my sister on the cheek. 'What's wrong, girleen?'

'He won't let me see Daddy Moo-Moo.'

'Will he not?' she said as she lifted Lucy out of my arms. 'Isn't he the bold boy? Let's just look at him through the gate.'

Lucy smiled triumphantly.

Maybe I'm being uptight, I thought to myself. *All she wants to do is look at him. He's never going to eat grass out of her hand anyway.*

That proved to be the case – the bull just ignored them.

Shortly afterwards, the rain – a fine drizzly mist – came down and we had to retreat indoors. Mrs Baker served up tea and cake.

'I heard on the news this morning that all's set for the launch on Wednesday,' she informed me. 'You must come down and watch it. It'll be broadcast live in the afternoon.'

'Thank you. I will,' I said.

Before I left, I told Eilis I'd catch up with her if she was going to the creamery the next morning.

'I'll be there,' she said.

'Maybe we could find that movie set?' I asked.

Eilis nodded. 'We'll take the bikes.'

Later in the day, though, I met her again. The rain had cleared and I'd gone to the beach with Mom and Lucy. I was out surfing, and Mom and Lucy had wandered off, when she came riding on Lir down to the beach.

I kept on with what I was doing. I'd already caught a couple of waves and was feeling confident. As I paddled into position for another one, I saw Eilis dismount and walk her horse to the water's edge.

Uh-oh, here she comes – don't make a fool of yourself, Danny, I thought.

The wave came too, a big one. I caught it. Away we went, as Mom would say, 'on a wing and a prayer'.

I don't want to exaggerate. With a homemade board like mine, which is only a plank, you can't 'angle' a wave or try anything fancy; it's just a matter of staying up there and riding it straight to shore. The surfing may be short but it's sweet.

And it was sweet, riding that wave … until the last moment, that is, when the wave closed over and I was thrown. Nothing unusual, only this time the plank smacked me on the forehead, just over the eye. I'd never been whacked on the head by a plank before. It hurt.

'You're bleeding!' Eilis cried as I stumbled out of the water, dragging the plank behind me.

'It's nothing,' I said, wiping my forehead.

'Wait here,' she commanded. 'You too, Lir.'

The horse did as he was told as well, while she ran away towards the rock pools. Presently she returned with a clump of red seaweed. 'Here, this'll do it good,' she said, holding the back of my head as she pressed the seaweed on the cut. 'You poor boy. Is it sore?'

'Nah,' I said, which wasn't exactly true.

'Well, this seaweed has the healing. You'll be as right as rain.'

Her hands felt warm against my head. I was beginning to shiver with the cold, though, and my forehead was stinging. It also felt a bit weird having seaweed stuck to my face, but kind of good too.

'That's surfing for you,' I said. 'Would you'd like to try?'

'Sure,' she said gamely.

'Are you serious?'

'I'll try surfing if you try riding my horse again,' she replied.

I pondered it a moment.

'Okay, it's a deal,' I said. 'You know what? I'll even make a surfboard for you.'

Eilis turned to her horse. 'What do you think of that, Lir? He says he'll make a surfboard for us.'

The horse snickered quietly.

I laughed. 'Do you guys talk to each other?'

Then Mom arrived on the scene, saw the blood and pitched a fit, saying I'd have to go to the doctor, while Lucy grabbed hold of me, crying, 'Danny's hurt his head! Danny's hurt his head!'

It was *so* embarrassing.

Amazingly, the seaweed worked. When Eilis took her hand away, the bleeding had almost stopped and Mom soon calmed down. 'That's enough surfing today, young man,' she said.

'It's nothin', Mom,' I groaned.

'That plank's dangerous,' she insisted. 'You can't go back surfing with that thing.'

'All I need to do is get Grandpa to smooth it off some more,' I replied.

Mom shook her head and said nothing.

I left the board back in the grass hollow and got dressed, after saying goodbye to Eilis. I figured it might be best to give surfing a rest for a day or two.

As we drove home past the Bakers' place, she was outside, sitting on the wall. She was chatting to two boys about my age. I waved as we went by, but she didn't notice.

'Eilis is very popular,' Mom remarked.

'I don't know what you mean,' I said.

'Only joking,' said Mom.

Grandpa pulled my leg too. 'Did you meet Muhammad Ali on your way home?' he asked as soon as we walked in the kitchen.

'I got punched by a heavyweight surfboard,' I sighed.

'Should I bring him to the doctor?' said Mam. 'He might need a stitch.'

'Ah sure, that's not even a scratch!' Grandpa said.

In his slow, measured way he stepped over to the big closet, peered inside and started examining the contents. After a few seconds he took out a small brown bottle. Holding it up to the light he gave it a small shake.

'What's that?' I asked anxiously.

'Just a little something,' he said, placing the bottle on the table. 'Just a little something.'

Grandpa pulled out a drawer – in the most unhurried way you could ever pull out a drawer – and tore a small wad of cotton wool off a big roll. Taking the bottle in his massive farmer's hand, he opened it with a slow and squeaky turn of the cork. He put down the cork, took up the wad of cotton and pressed it to the mouth of the bottle. 'Come here, boy,' he said.

'Is this some kind of rattlesnake potion?' I enquired.

'Tilt your head,' he commanded, shaking the bottle.

I was close enough to smell the stuff and, boy, it hit me straight in the nostrils. It was a sharp, chemical kind of smell.

His voice was sharp too. 'Keep still now.'

I didn't quite like the way things were shaping up and, sure enough, when he pressed the cotton on my cut it felt like I'd been stung by a platoon of vicious bees.

I sprang away. 'Ouch! What is that stuff?'

Lucy was staring at me with her mouth open.

'What? Are you a man or a mouse?' asked my grandfather, his smiling blue eyes following me as I hopped around the floor, grimacing with the pain. 'Don't cover that – let the air get at it,' he said and he strolled from the kitchen.

'That was mean,' Lucy whispered. 'Danny's face is all brown!'

'Grandpa's trying to make Danny better, that's all,' said Mom.

'What's in that bottle?' I asked.

'Iodine,' she whispered. 'He used to treat us with it when we were kids.'

Later I had to admit that, between the seaweed and the iodine, my wound felt much better.

19

'You've been in the wars, haven't you?' the lady in the village post office said as I laid out my money on the counter.

'Yep,' I sighed. I had looked in a mirror, and that ugly yellow-brown stain on my forehead from Grandpa's potion made me look like Frankenstein's monster.

It was 4.30 on Monday afternoon and I was about to phone Jimmy. I'd left it late – the post office would close in half an hour – because by my reckoning it was only about 10 a.m. back home.

The heap of coins was confusing to me, so I accepted her help in counting them out. She pointed to the booth with the glass door. 'Step inside and I'll try to connect you.'

The phone was a big, black ancient thing with an arm at the side for winding. I picked up the receiver. The line was dead. I waited. Nothing happened. So I stuck my head out the door and asked: 'Do I have to wind the arm?'

'Of course,' she replied.

I wound the arm but nothing happened.

'You must be winding it the wrong way round!' she shouted.

I couldn't wait to talk to Jimmy. I stood there tapping my feet on the floorboards. My head wasn't sore any more but my hands were. They were blistered from working on the Bakers' farm that morning. After another hair-raising ride to the creamery, I hoped we might cycle to the set of *Ryan's Daughter*. But Eilis had to turn the hay again with her father and brothers so I offered to help.

'You may pick up the receiver now,' the lady called out from behind the counter.

The line was all buzzy. Then I heard the same lady's musical voice. 'Go ahead, Florida, your caller's on the line.'

'Hey, are you there, Danny?' came Jimmy's faraway voice.

'Yep, it's me,' I hollered.

'How's it goin' over there in Ireland, Danny Boy?'

We talked excitedly. He told me about the surfing in Daytona and I told him I was surfing too. That impressed him and he started quizzing me about it – about my board and the waves. I knew time was running out.

'Hey, Jimmy.' I cut to the chase. 'How's it going with Apollo over there?'

The question ignited him like rocket fuel. 'Oh, wait, wait, that's what I wanted to tell you … Linda Palmer, right? Well, I don't know did you know this, but her dad is a reporter and – can you believe it? – he's got special passes for the launch on Wednesday!'

'Good for her,' I said.

'But wait for this – wait for this, Danny – she's invited me and Gloria Romero along too. We're going to the lift off, man! Lots of the other guys are going down there too, like Bobby Schultz, Tom Ritchie, Kate Brown – in fact, everyone's going down – but they'll be watching from the beaches and highways like everyone else whereas,' he sang it out, 'we'll be in the press area!'

'That's great, Jimmy,' I said, feeling like I'd just been punched in the stomach. 'You'll be able to get great material for the project. Okay, buddy?'

'That's what I wanted to talk to you about,' said Danny. He paused.

'Hi, Jimmy?'

'Yeah, I was wondering, Danny … How'd you feel if Linda joined us on the project?'

I took a deep breath. This had come out of left field. 'I don't know about that,' I said.

'And maybe Gloria too?'

I said nothing.

'They are "Go" for this project, Danny. You know the way girls are. They work harder and do stuff more carefully than us. We can win it with them, hands-down.'

'Four's too much,' I said.

'Mr Walker said there's no limit on numbers.'

'I don't know.' I hesitated.

'Besides,' said Jimmy, 'I think Gloria Romero likes you, Danny.'

'What's all this about?' I said.

'It's true.'

'Who says so?'

'I say so.'

'No, you don't,' I said. 'I know what's going on here.'

'What going on?'

'And it's got nothing to do with Gloria Romero liking Danny Sullivan,' I added. 'It's about you liking Linda Palmer! Am I right or am I right? That's what's going on here!'

Jimmy laughed quietly. 'Hey, I bet you're sweet-talking all those girls in Ireland,' he replied, trying to turn the tables.

'Who? Me? No way.'

'You have thirty seconds left,' the post-office lady's voice broke into the line.

I needed to get my friend back on track, fast.

'Listen, Jimmy. If you get to the press area, there's sure to be loads of pamphlets, leaflets, pin badges, buttons, stickers, that kind of stuff. Make sure to get them all.'

'You can count on me,' said Jimmy sweetly.

'In fact, get two of everything.'

'Will do.'

'Good.'

'So, are you okay with Linda and Gloria?'

'Let's see how it goes,' I said. 'I don't mind if we win this project with two or four as long–'

'It's time up now,' the lady cut in again.

'As long as we win,' I added.

'Okay, I'll be seeing you,' said Jimmy.

'I'll be watching out for you on the TV,' I said as the line went dead.

I thanked the lady and left.

This project was a mess. I had done little or no work and knew Jimmy had done nothing either. Now it looked like Linda Palmer and Gloria Romero were getting involved. Of course, that could be wishful thinking on Jimmy's part. Just because he might ask them to join us didn't mean they would. Not only were Linda and Gloria best friends, they always got straight As. They might want to do their own project.

Once girls get involved, things get complicated, I said to myself.

It's not a long walk home from the village. The road runs straight for a couple of hundred yards, then you come to a sharp corner with the turn off to the beach just before the Bakers' place, then the entrance to my grandfather's farm a bit further down on the right. When I swung around that corner, whistling a tune to myself, who did I see only those two guys talking to Eilis again. Two other girls sat on the wall nearby, both with long brown hair. I didn't know whether to stop and talk or just keep on walking.

'Hi,' I managed as I went past.

'Danny Sullivan, come over here and say hello,' Eilis replied.

I wheeled around.

'This is Barry and Paul, from Dublin – but we won't hold that against them. They're here in the college learning Irish.'

'Hi,' I repeated.

They nodded but said nothing.

'And that's Rose and Joanna,' said Eilis. They giggled. It all felt a bit awkward and I didn't feel like hanging around.

'Danny's from Florida in the USA,' Eilis told them. 'Danny, do you know there's a sports day in the college tomorrow afternoon and the lads have invited us. Do you want to come?'

'Maybe,' I replied with a shrug.

Eilis turned to the two boys. 'That's okay with you, lads, isn't it?'

'Suppose so,' muttered Barry, while his friend, the one with the slicked-back hair, sniggered.

Another awkward silence. I didn't really like those two guys.

'I guess I'd better go,' I said. 'S'long for now.'

The girls on the wall gave a little wave as I walked away.

'Are you coming to the creamery in the morning?' Eilis called after me.

'Yeah, maybe,' I replied over my shoulder.

What did I tell you, Danny? I thought as I walked up the bohereen. *Once girls step into the frame, things get complicated.*

20

I messed up.

To begin with, I should have remembered those bedtime stories my dad used to tell me – the ones about foxes. It was really just the same fox story told over and over again with a few changes here and there. Always a farm on a hillside, the farmer living alone and lots of chickens. Nearby lived a fox, a very hungry fox with a hungry family to feed. On a moonlit night – it was always so – the fox came prowling. He would cross fields, ditches, a stream, more fields, coming closer and closer. The fox would sneak up to the chicken house … and find the door left open.

I should have remembered that.

Exhausted by the farm work, I could barely stay awake after dinner. Then I went to bed early, my legs aching as I dragged them up the creaky stairs. I climbed into bed and fell fast asleep.

A noise woke me, the sound of furious flapping. When you're suddenly woken in the middle of the night, there's something scary about it, something unreal, as if you're still dreaming. I didn't move for a moment. I just lay there. Until I heard the sharp squawk of a frightened hen.

I sprang from my bed and stared out the window.

It was the weirdest sight. Below in the yard, five or six hens were perched on top of the hedge flapping their wings like crazy.

The fox was standing on her hind legs, with front paws scrabbling at the hedge. She looked ready to spring – or perhaps even to climb up the hedge.

Oh man, the door, I thought. *You forgot the door.*

'Go away!' I roared and banged the window. The fox whipped around and shot away.

As I flew downstairs I heard Grandpa getting out of bed. When I ran outside I saw feathers scattered on the grass. The hens were still on top of the hedge, pitching around like crazy puppets as they tried to keep their balance.

Then Grandpa appeared with a pitchfork. He was dressed only in long johns and wearing hobnail boots. His eyes were aflame. He looked scary.

'It's the fox,' I told him, which I guess was a dumb thing to say.

He swept by me.

Mom came out. 'Oh dear,' she groaned, eyeing the feathers on the grass and all those chickens on the hedge, clucking like crazy.

I climbed onto the stone wall and looked around. There was no moon but in the midnight blue you could see the sheep at rest, the silent fields and the mountains in silhouette.

A short while later Grandpa came back holding a very dead hen by the legs. He slammed the pitchfork into the ground and dropped the bird nearby. Then, without a word, he disappeared into the shadows again.

Mom and I set about trying to catch hens. We caught some on the hedge with a quick grab, but some shot into the field and a couple went scurrying around the garden. I gulped when I saw the open door of the hen house and remembered those eggs I had collected earlier in the evening.

I forgot to shut the door, I thought. *Grandpa will be mad at me.*

Mom looked at the door, then at me, and shrugged.

'I'm sorry,' I whispered.

'Don't worry, he won't mind. We'll have lovely roast chicken for dinner tomorrow, Danny.'

'That's not funny, Mom,' I replied.

Grandpa reappeared, this time with Kerry. The dog looked agitated. I wanted to say something but I couldn't find the words.

Finally, we got the chickens back in their house, at least as far as we could tell. Grandpa pulled the door shut and lowered the latch.

He turned and looked me in the eye. 'That door is shut and it stays shut.'

I nodded and said nothing.

21

I knew there'd be hell to pay.

I'd only known my grandfather a week, but I understood him. He was Ireland's answer to Clint Eastwood: fair in his dealings but deadly when crossed.

In the Wild West the lowest, meanest son-of-a-gun was the rustler. The rustler stole cattle from the honest, hard-working cowboy. If there was a rustler in the county, you'd put a bounty on his head and send for the posse, or Clint. Clint knew how to deal with bad guys. He'd take care of them ...

That fox had turned rustler. Now she would have to pay for stealing the farmer's chickens. That was the law.

I couldn't get back to sleep thinking about it.

Sure, I was mad at the fox for doing what she'd done, mad at her for getting me into trouble. But it wasn't her fault. She was born to hunt and she had hungry mouths to feed. What else could she do? Go to the supermarket?

Though my dad had grown up on a farm, he used to like foxes. I knew that from his stories. He'd thought foxes were cool. They were the Robin Hoods of the animal world: brave, smart hunters who lived by their wits.

Dad's fox stories always ended with a hunt. The farmer and his friends, with their horses and their ferocious dogs, would come after the rustler. But the fox would out-fox them. Whether by diving into a river or disappearing into a cave, the fox would always escape.

But they were just stories, make-believe.

If I had kept that door shut, none of this would have happened. It was my fault. My grandfather wanted revenge. And if – when – that fox died, what would happen to her cubs?

Dawn had broken by the time I fell asleep.

I woke in a daze and reached for my watch. It said: 11.05. *You missed that ride to the creamery – again*, I told myself. Then I remembered the chickens and my heart sank.

I heard Lucy singing outside, and when I looked out the window I saw her sitting on a blanket in the sunshine, playing with her dolls.

My grandfather came into view in the field below, his dog alongside him. The sheep began to shift, some getting up on their feet, others walking away. All it took was a gesture, a wave of the hand from Grandpa, and Kerry swung into action. The round-up had begun.

I dressed and went downstairs.

Mom was standing by the sink. I couldn't believe what I was seeing – she was plucking the chicken.

'I'm not eating that for dinner,' I said. 'No way.'

'Come on, Danny, you eat chicken all the time!'

'This is different,' I said. 'This chicken is different.'

'How is it different?'

'It just is,' I said.

I didn't feel like breakfast either. I knew I had to talk with my grandfather first. I had to bite the bullet. So all I had was a cup of tea, which I was getting used to drinking over here. Then I went outside.

'Danny, I want to give Hello his bottle,' Lucy called as I crossed the yard.

'Okay, follow me,' I said.

Grandpa had already penned the sheep. Kerry was standing nearby, awaiting orders.

'Good morning,' I said.

'Good morning, Grandpa,' Lucy echoed in her squeaky voice.

He nodded to me and gave the thumbs-up to Lucy. He was standing among the sheep with some kind of spray-bottle in his hand.

'What's the bottle for?' I said, trying to make conversation.

'To dose them,' he replied. He made no further explanation.

Suddenly he pounced on a sheep. Grabbing its fleece with just one hand and simultaneously clamping the animal with his legs – an amazing feat of strength given my grandfather's age – he pried its mouth open with the nozzle of the bottle and gave it a 'dose' of medicine or whatever it was. Then he put down the bottle, picked up a brush from what looked like a bucket of paint or dye and daubed a blue X on the animal.

'I could help you with that,' I offered.

'I won't say no,' he replied. 'I'm getting too old for this kind of caper.'

I climbed into the pen. He passed me the bottle.

'Have you come to say hello to Hello?' he asked my sister.

'He wants his breakfast,' she replied shyly.

'Well, he's hiding here, do you see him?'

'He's in the corner!' Lucy exclaimed, pointing out her pet.

With that, Grandpa pounced on another woolly fellow.

'Now, give him a shot of that,' he said when he'd subdued the animal.

'Do they bite?' I asked.

'Not at all,' he scoffed. 'They wouldn't bite if you paid them.'

With that he pried the mouth open and I could see the row of small, blunt teeth. There wasn't one fang among them. I delivered the dose.

'Good man,' said my grandfather. He daubed the sheep with blue, released it and edged towards the next one.

'I'm sorry for leaving the door open,' I began.

'No bother,' he replied quietly.

'But you lost a chicken.'

'Two.' He pushed the cap back on his head and gave me that half-smile. 'That fox is the cute one. She hid one below in the field and came back for the second.'

'That's terrible,' I said.

Immediately he pounced upon another sheep and we went through the procedure once more.

When that was over and he was sizing up the next, I said, 'I guess you'll do something about it.'

'I'll deal with it the way we've always dealt with it,' he answered.

'Look, it's my fault,' I went on. 'What d'you say if I pay you for the chickens and you let the fox –' I paused to reformulate the words - 'you don't kill her?'

He looked at me as if I was mad. 'Are you pulling my leg?'

'I am not, sir,' I answered.

He shook his head in disbelief. 'The answer is no.'

'The cubs,' I blurted out. 'Are you going to kill them too?'

'I've no quarrel with any cubs ... as long as they stay away from my hens.'

'But if you kill the mother, what will happen to them?' I pleaded.

'She has to go.'

I knew it was pointless to argue.

After the sheep were dosed, Lucy gave Hello his bottle, and I went up to the old house where the timber was stored. I wanted to make a board for Eilis, but I didn't want to ask my grandfather to help. So I borrowed his tools and set to work.

Were it not for the fox, the day would have been perfect. The sun was high and the larks were singing out of the blue dome of the sky. Outside the door, in the grassy farmyard, gold and white wildflowers trembled in the soft breeze. As I measured and sawed, I kept watch for a pair of swallows that would suddenly appear out of nowhere – over the bushes on my right one minute, swerving round from the left the next – to dart in and out of the other tumble-down shed.

I tried to focus on the board, which I was making out of another piece of plank – this one lighter than the last. The hardest part was the planing. I had to be sure there were no edges left on this plank, that everything was smooth and curved, because I wouldn't want to see Eilis getting injured like me.

The chickens were out and about in the yard but looked quite wary. *That fox brought this all down on herself. She deserves what she gets. Why should it bother me?* I thought.

Then I looked towards the outcrop of rock in the fields below and imagined the cubs playing in the sun, watched by their mother. Maybe the dad fox was there as well. All of them together like one big happy family.

And then I felt bad, real bad.

I can't let my grandfather do this. I've got to stop him.

But how?

I needed to talk to Eilis and ask her help. I wondered if she'd gone to that sports day. I hoped she hadn't.

By 3 p.m. I was done with the surfboard.

With the plane in one hand and the board in the other, I headed over to her place. There was nobody at the house. I went around the back and spotted Eilis's dad and her brother, Mike, in the field. They were raking the hay and gathering it into small haystacks about three-foot high.

Mike waved when he saw me at the gate.

'Have you seen Eilis?' I called out.

'I thought she went up to you a short while ago,' he answered.

I shrugged, puzzled. Mom and Lucy had left for the beach an hour earlier. Had Eilis called to the house and missed me?

I carried her board down to the hollow near the beach. Then I used the plane to smooth off mine some more and when that was done I left both boards there.

I'd decided to give the surfing a miss today and try out the snorkel and fins Mom had bought me. She and Lucy had gone to the small sandy cove I had crossed on my first morning in Kerry.

When I arrived, Lucy was trying to fill a hole with water and Mom was sketching. If you were looking for something to sketch, you'd find nothing better: the light blue sky over a deep blue sea, the headland with three identical hills on one side, Mount Brandon on the other, with a little fishing village in between, a mile across the bay.

'Help me, Danny,' Lucy asked before I had even sat down.

'I will,' I said. 'Let me try out these swim fins first.'

'Mommy, Danny won't help,' she complained.

'He will, honey, just as soon as he's had a swim,' said Mom.

Off I went. Boy was that water cold! It was deep and crystal clear by the rocks. There were no fish, but you could see the long strands of greeny-brown seaweed, ripples of sunlight playing on the sand and a couple of big relaxed-looking crabs, stuff like that. But the water was *freezing*!

After getting out and shivering in a towel for five minutes, I started filling buckets of water for Lucy's 'swimming pool'.

I told Mom about the deal I tried to make with Grandpa to save the fox's life. She laughed, which kind of bugged me. I didn't think it was funny. Not one bit.

22

'Where were you, boy?'

'Where were you?' I replied.

'I called for you but there was no-one there.'

'I was in the shed,' I said, 'making your surfboard.'

Eilis's frown melted away. 'So that's where you were!'

'Yep.'

We had met on Grandpa's bohereen as I was heading to her place and she to mine. Dusk had fallen. The air was still and tiny moths flitted silently along the hedgerow.

'And where are you off to now?'

I shrugged. 'Someplace. And you?'

'I'm going up to you, eejit!'

'Eejit? What's that?'

'Are you cross?'

'No,' I lied. 'How was sports day?'

'Grand. Pity you couldn't come,' she answered.

I said nothing.

'So, do you want to go to the film set tomorrow?'

'They're launching *Apollo* tomorrow.'

'I know,' she said. 'Couldn't we go earlier in the morning?'

'I can't,' I said. 'Look, I need to tell you something.'

I explained about the fox and the hens, all in a big rush. I had almost finished when Eilis gave me a nudge.

'Speak of the devil!' she laughed.

I looked behind me and saw Grandpa approaching in his

usual unhurried manner, pushing the big black bicycle. We exchanged hellos as he passed and I spotted a long stick-like shape that was wrapped in an old sack and strapped to the crossbar.

'He's got a rifle,' Eilis hissed.

'You're kidding!' I replied.

'There's gonna be a shoot-out at the OK Corral,' she whispered in a terrible American accent.

'No way,' I said.

'Try stopping him!' she exclaimed.

'I've an idea,' I said.

It was crazy, but I ran it by her anyway.

'Are you serious?' she gasped. Then she laughed. 'Well, I'm up for it if you are.'

'We've nothing to lose,' I said.

'No, except everyone will think we're the biggest eejits in Kerry. Or they'll think he is!'

I shrugged.

She looked me in the eye. 'There's just one snag.'

'What's that?'

'He could be loading up that gun right now.'

'You're kidding. He can't go shooting now, in the dark!'

'Why not? Isn't that when the fox is about?'

'I'd better go,' I said. 'I'll see you tomorrow.'

I ran up to the house. Lifting the door-latch quietly, I stepped inside. I could hear Mom's voice upstairs telling Lucy her bedtime story. There was no sign of Grandpa, but the sack lay on the kitchen table, next to the remains of the roast chicken. Yes, I'd had it for dinner, because it was either that or watch everyone else eat it.

Suddenly the backdoor opened. Grandpa came in clutching a large rusty biscuit tin and a rod tucked under his arm.

'Is it yourself?' he asked.

'I think so,' I replied and tried to make a joke out of it by feeling my arms, chest and legs to check if they were there. *Strange question,* I thought.

'And where's herself?'

'She had to go,' I said. Then I added, 'She figured there might be a few bullets flying.'

He laughed quietly. 'She may be right, she may be right.'

I filled the kettle at the sink. 'So, when are you going a-hunting?' I asked as nonchalantly as I could.

'Tomorrow evening. I've to clean this gun first.'

'Would you like a cup of tea?' I enquired.

'If you're making it.'

I cleared the table as he tried to untie a knot in the cord around the sack. 'Blast you,' he muttered darkly, his giant fingers fumbling.

'Here, let me do it,' I offered.

He handed it to me. The gun in the sack felt heavy. I untied the knot and handed it back. Without removing the weapon from the sack, he put it down on the table again.

'A neighbour borrowed the gun, and I've only got it back today. It'll need a good clean.' He removed a number of items from the tin: a small brush; a toothbrush; a pair of needle-nosed pliers; a small can of oil and a bottle of solvent. Then he left the room.

I made the pot of tea and poured him a cup.

He returned with a cotton sheet and a scissors and set about cutting a large square from the sheet. Then he cut a smaller patch from it.

I sipped my tea and watched, mesmerised, as he cut more patches and placed them one top of the other on the table. Finally, I blurted out my question: 'Can I come with you? When you go hunting?'

He gave me a penetrating look that seemed to say, *Why would you want to do that?*

'To make sure you get the cubs as well,' I added jokingly.

He winked at me once more. 'Maybe it's the bounty you're after?'

'What bounty?'

'The fox bounty. If you bring the fox's tail to the guards, they'll pay you a bounty for it.'

'The police? You're not serious,' I said.

'They will pay you,' he insisted.

Having laid out his gun-cleaning kit, he picked up the sack once more. 'Maybe you should go and see what your mother's doing upstairs,' he said.

I took the hint. I needed to talk with Mom anyway.

I tiptoed up the stairs and found her asleep in the bed with Lucy. This often happened to Mom when she tried to get Lucy to sleep – she'd nod off herself, she'd be so tired. The only problem was if she slept now she wouldn't be able to sleep later.

I shook her shoulder gently. 'Mom!'

She sat up and yawned. 'Hi, Danny.'

'Like a cup of tea?'

'No, thank you.'

I filled her in on what Grandpa was doing downstairs.

'Stay away from that gun, hear me?' she whispered. 'He doesn't want you near it.'

'I won't touch it, promise,' I said. 'Listen, Mom, I've something to ask you. Can you do me a favour?'

'Like what?'

'Remember you said you were going to town to buy Grandpa a refrigerator? Could you do that tomorrow? Like, early in the morning?'

She looked at me, puzzled. 'Why?'

'Because I want to come along.'

'But why?'

'I need to get something. And here's another thing, could you loan me a couple of dollars – I mean pounds?'

'What for, Danny?'

'I'll tell you tomorrow. Just promise me we'll go to Tralee?'

'Okay,' she said, ruffling my hair.

'Mom, you're cool,' I said.

When I came back downstairs, the kitchen was empty. Grandpa obviously wanted to clean his rifle in private.

By now it was dark outside. I was dog-tired and needed to sleep. But do you think I could? My body was beat but my mind was spinning. I thought of my crazy plan to save the fox. I thought about *Apollo 11* and its crew, blasting into the unknown. I thought of my classmates going to Cape Kennedy. I was going to miss the biggest thing ever.

My mind raced from one worry to the next.

Out of nowhere, a little song that Dad used to sing popped into my mind. It was one of his favourites on long car journeys and sometimes we'd all sing along.

> *Run rabbit, run rabbit,*
> *Run, run, run.*
> *Don't let the farmer get his*
> *Gun, gun, gun.*
> *He'll get by*
> *Without his rabbit pie,*
> *So, run rabbit, run rabbit,*
> *Run, run, run.*

Little did I know then that stuff like that happened in real life.

23

Mr Walker knew about Apollo launches. He had witnessed the *Apollo 8* lift-off in December and he told us all about it.

When Mr Walker spoke, everyone listened. The day he stood beside his Saturn V model and talked about *Apollo 8*, you could hear a pin drop.

'That night, down on Pad 39-A, this baby was lit up by floodlights – you could see it eight miles away,' he began in his slightly hoarse voice. 'Overnight, while the crew slept, they filled these enormous tanks here with liquid oxygen.' He tapped each of the three stages with his pen. 'This "lox" has a temperature of 290 degrees below zero and it hisses and wails as it runs through the pipes. They poured a half a million gallons of it and kerosene into the first stage alone.'

Greg Meyer, who was sitting just behind me, gasped in disbelief.

'It's a highly flammable material, with almost enough power to explode like an atomic bomb,' added our teacher.

Linda Palmer put up her hand. Mr Walker gave her a nod.

'What if something went wrong?' she asked.

'Well, Linda, that would very bad news ... First of all, everyone is kept well back, at least three and a half miles. And, less than a mile from the pad, there's a line of armoured-plated tanks waiting to help if there's an emergency.'

Linda had her hand in the air again. 'Yes, Linda?' said Mr Walker.

'But what about the astronauts?'

'Remember, they're going to be strapped in, seated in their spacecraft at the very top of the rocket here,' he replied. 'If something goes wrong – and if they have enough time – they can do one of two things. First, there's a slide wire that runs all the way from the top of the launch tower to a reinforced bunker at the bottom. They'll need to get down there fast. That's one option. But there mightn't be enough time for that. That's why there's a small escape rocket right on top of the command module's nose. Up here.' He gave it one crisp tap with his pen. 'The astronauts fire this rocket and – bombs away – they're catapulted into the sky and safety. But it's a very dangerous manoeuvre and not one you ever want to have to resort to, Linda.'

'I've been thinking, Mom,' I said as we drove towards Tralee.

'About what?' said Mom. She had chosen another route over the mountains to avoid that scary pass we had come through ten days earlier. We were descending now and far below you could see a white line of breakers sweeping onto a beach. I figured it was the same beach I had noticed the day we arrived.

'I don't think I'd like to be an astronaut after all.'

She glanced in the mirror. 'I see.'

'Surfer, yes. Astronaut, no,' I said. 'But Mr Walker would make a good astronaut.'

'I guess he would,' said Mom. 'Calm under pressure. You're lucky to have him as a teacher.'

'No, I'm not. He gives big homework assignments,' I replied.

'But you guys don't seem to mind – like this Apollo project you're working on.'

'That's only because we want to win the Saturn Five model

and the VIP tour,' I said. 'But I can't do it here anyway.' That really bugged me. I loved it in Kerry, but I'd give anything to be in Florida right now, today, with Apollo about to blast off for the moon. Instead I was here trying to stop my crazy grandpa from killing a fox!

'Mommy, I've got a headache in my head,' Lucy spoke up. She had been sitting quietly beside me the whole time, which was unusual.

'I hope you're not coming down with anything, honey,' said Mom.

'My throat hurts too, Mommy,' she complained. 'Want to see, Danny?' She opened up her mouth and I leaned over and peered in.

'Hey, those tonsils are big!' I observed.

Lucy sniffed and gave a little cry.

'You poor wee scrap,' said Mom. 'We'll go straight to the drugstore and get you something for that.'

'And Danny,' Lucy said, looking at me with those big sad eyes, 'will you bring me to see Daddy Moo-Moo when we get home?'

'Sure,' I said. *What a great actress*, I thought.

We parked the car on a street in town. I asked Mom for the keys to the trunk and told her I'd meet her here in fifteen minutes.

She raised an eyebrow. 'You still haven't told me what you're up to.'

'You'll see,' I said as I skipped off down the street.

Nothing had changed in the Kingdom of Curio. Like someone caught in a time warp, the guy with the moustache was still sitting there, reading his newspaper. It had *The Kerryman* written on the front page in funny letters. He gave a friendly nod when I entered.

'Are you enjoying the holiday?'

'Sure thing!'

I sidled over to the stuffed fox. 'Sir, how much is this?'

He paused and put down his newspaper. 'Five pounds and fifteen shillings,' he announced.

'Would you let me have it for five?'

His eyes widened. 'Yerra, what would you want it for?'

'It's kind of a long story.' I grinned sheepishly.

'Will you bring it home with you? Stuff it in a suitcase, like?'

'No, sir.'

'Is it a present for someone?'

I nodded.

'Might I ask for whom?'

'My grandfather.'

'Oh, I see. Is he a Kerryman, your grandfather? I mean, he's not from Cork or anywhere?'

'He's definitely from Kerry,' I confirmed.

'Good, good. Well, if that's the case,' he said and paused for what seemed like a long time. 'If that's the case, we'll have to let you have this fine specimen of an Irish fox for five pounds.'

'Thank you,' I said. I put down four pound notes on the counter and began counting out the remainder in coins, while he went looking for wrapping paper.

This is costing me. It better work, I thought.

He put the thing in a huge brown-paper bag and taped it shut. 'Tell me, how's the little sister?' he enquired.

'She's fine,' I said.

He handed one of the big silver coins back to me, the one they call the half-crown. 'Here, take this and buy her an ice-cream.'

I thanked him again and lifted the bulky bag. He opened the door for me and we said goodbye.

It wasn't easy carrying a stuffed fox down the street. It was heavy and, from snout to outstretched tail, it must have been over a yard long. I hurried back to the car. *Apollo 11* was due to lift-off at 2.30 p.m., Irish time, and it was 10.35 a.m. already.

Mom and Lucy were waiting for me. Mom held a bottle of medicine and Lucy licked an ice-cream. *Some sore throat she has,* I thought.

'What have you got there?' Mom asked, eyeing the package as I put it in the trunk.

As we made our way to the electrical store, I told her my plan. 'He's going to shoot that fox this evening,' I whispered, so Lucy would not hear. 'But when he goes down, he'll see this fox standing on the boulders instead. Grandpa will blast it to high heaven. I'll bring back the tail and Grandpa will get his fox bounty from the police. Job done. Simple as that.'

Mom shook her head.

'So what do you think, Mom?'

'What makes you think that will fool him?' she said. 'He has a pair of eyes, you know.'

'This is a real stuffed fox, Mom. It would fool anyone,' I said. 'It'll be almost dark. And because it'll be high up on the rocks, I'll climb up and fetch it for him.'

'So you're planning to go shooting with him?' asked Mom, making a face.

'I'll be careful, I promise.'

'You're not to shoot the fox, Danny!' Lucy snapped at me. Small sisters have big ears and big mouths, in my experience.

'I won't, Lucy,' I assured her.

'I don't like you making a fool out of him either,' Mom added.

'C'mon, Mom,' I pleaded. 'I'm trying to save a fox, a mother to three tiny cubs.'

'He's your grandfather, Danny.'

'Yeah, but he's got a sense of humour,' I insisted. 'If he finds out, he'll just laugh.'

'I hope so,' Mom said, 'for your sake.' Then she looked at me and laughed. 'You're exactly like your father: a chancer! That's just the kind of thing he'd have done.'

I was glad to hear her say that.

'Now, we'd better find that electrical store,' Mom said.

You might think that buying a refrigerator is simple. Not so. We looked at every make and model in that store – twice over. Mom leafed through the manual of each machine and examined the customer guarantee. Then she started discussing the price. It all took forever. Then we went to a few more stores and had an early lunch. By the time we got back to the car it was 1.05 p.m. and my heart was racing.

24

My game plan almost fell apart when we got back to the farm.

With so little time to lift-off, I was rushing to get to the Bakers'. Mom needed me to unpack the car and she asked to see the stuffed fox. I handed Lucy something to bring into the house and then pulled the big bag open in the car trunk to give Mom a peep. I wondered whether I should sneak down to the Bakers' place and hide it in their barn.

Suddenly, I heard my grandfather ask Lucy, 'And what have you got there, Missy?'

Mom had hysterics and I panicked, folding the bag back over the fox's freaky head. Only the open lid of the trunk saved Grandpa from seeing it as he came round the corner of the house.

I bundled the thing back in and slammed the trunk shut. Mom was trying really hard not to laugh.

'We've got a present for you, Grandpa,' Lucy said, taking him by the hand.

'A little bottle of something,' said Mom, wiping her brow in a theatrical manner. 'Isn't that right, Danny?'

Mom had bought a small bottle of whiskey for him, but it was in the trunk. For obvious reasons, I wasn't about to give it to him now. 'Oh, yeah, yeah,' I said.

'Will you bring me to see the fairies? Please, Grandpa?' Lucy requested.

The old man pushed back the cap on his head and grinned. 'The fairies are too busy mending shoes at the moment.'

'And, honey, we have to see the rocket going to the moon,' Mom reminded her.

'I don't want to. I want to see fairies,' Lucy protested.

'Well, you've more chance of seeing fairies than a man on the moon,' said Grandpa.

'You should come to the Bakers' and watch it on TV,' I said, regaining my composure.

'Maybe, maybe,' he said.

I didn't think he would, though.

I can't say I was cool, calm and collected by the time I got to Eilis's house. I was sweating, for sure, and it wasn't because of the sun.

'We thought you'd never arrive,' Mrs Baker greeted me at the door. She ushered me into the living room. Eilis, Sean and Mike were sitting on the carpet in front of the television. Two friends of Mike's, Ciaran and Donal, and an elderly neighbour, Mrs O'Connor, were perched on the Bakers' sofa.

'Sit yourself down,' said Eilis. 'It's not long to lift-off.'

'They're live pictures,' Sean informed me.

I stared at the black-and-white TV screen. Across the lagoon on a bright Florida morning the majestic Saturn V stood on the launch pad, white plumes of vapour streaming from it.

I had cut it close. The clock at the bottom of the screen said:

MINS.   SECS.
-24   47
APOLLO COUNTDOWN

My pulse quickened.

The reporter in Florida was saying what a sweltering hot day it was and that a million people had come to view the launch. A million! The countdown was going perfectly, he said. But it was

120

hard to make out what he was saying against the buzz of the excited crowds and the loud NASA commentary on the tannoy.

I thought of Jimmy, Linda and Gloria and felt envious. They'd probably been up all night, having the time of their lives. Lots of others from school would be there too, on Cocoa beach and on the highways and access roads, waiting for that clock to tick to zero. You wouldn't need to be in the press area to view this giant blasting off – you'd see it from forty miles away.

'It's only nine in the morning over there,' said Sean.

Mrs Baker came back into the room and handed out bottles of soda and packets of potato chips to everyone. Then she brought in tea for herself and Mrs O'Connor.

'Did you sort out your business in Tralee?' Eilis whispered in my ear.

'Yeah, I'll tell you later,' I said. I wanted to focus on what was happening on the television. They had cut back to the studio where two guys began talking about the unfolding events.

I wondered if Mr Walker would be at the launch right now, and thought of what he'd told us in class.

'Upon ignition, the first thing you'll see are those yellow-orange flames and the huge clouds of vapour shooting out as all the fuel in the first stage is set alight. Everyone around you is on their feet, pumping their fists, cheering and roaring … It seems to take an age for this monster to clear the tower but it does. Don't forget, you're three and a half miles back and it's only now the sound rolls out … The birds out on the mudflats will bolt into the air … Then BANG! A tidal wave of sound will hit you full-on right here in the chest; your eardrums feel like they're going to burst; you can't hear the shouts from the people standing right next to you now; the heat-wave is intense; the ground is shaking …'

121

My mind returned to the room. Mom and Lucy arrived and Mrs Baker did all the introductions. More teas and soft drinks were handed out. It was hard to hear what they were saying on TV.

They had cut back to live pictures from a helicopter in Florida: roads jammed with cars and lined with people. 'And here comes the big Atlantic swell rolling onto the beaches,' said the reporter as the camera panned out over Cocoa Beach.

Look at the size of those waves, I thought with a pang. *You could be surfing right now ... surfing with Apollo taking off behind you ...*

Even the beach was crammed with cars. People were waving up to the helicopter. Signs were scrawled in the sand: 'Good luck *Apollo 11*'. Then the pictures returned to the awesome sight of the Saturn V on the launch pad.

I had no interest in soda or potato chips. I sat on the edge of my seat, transfixed.

'Sh-sh-sh-sh! I can't hear what the man is saying!' Sean complained. Everyone in the room, except me, laughed. I wanted them to hush too.

Mr Baker had come in and was standing quietly by the door. All over the world, hundreds of millions of people had gathered like us around their TV sets.

As the clock silently counted down, the room grew quiet. Lucy sat on Mom's lap, sipping her drink without a sound. Even the guys in the television studio had quit talking and had handed over commentary to the NASA man in the control centre.

'We've passed the six-minute mark on the countdown for *Apollo 11*,' he calmly informed the world.

The great swing arm connecting the top of the launch tower to the spacecraft now pulled away. Some hours earlier, Neil Armstrong, Buzz Aldrin and Michael Collins had walked across it and climbed into their command module. *If anything goes wrong at this point, they can only use the escape rocket*, I thought grimly.

'Two minutes thirty seconds and counting,' said the NASA man. 'We are still go on *Apollo 11* at this time.'

Sean gave a little yelp of excitement.

'I can't look,' Eilis whispered to me.

'Me too,' I said. I felt my stomach tightening.

Out across the lagoon, Saturn V stood waiting, exhaling white vapour like a shiny, breathing beast. I wished my grandfather had come down to watch this. He'd have to believe that the moon mission was real then.

'T minus sixty seconds and counting ...'

There was no turning back now. An image of Cocoa Beach flashed across my mind. I saw myself as a little kid, sitting on my dad's shoulders and gazing into the sky.

'Thirty seconds and counting ... The astronauts report, "It feels good."'

'God bless those men,' uttered Mrs O'Connor.

Mom had her eyes shut. I knew she was praying too.

'T minus fifteen seconds ... guidance is internal.'

The room was deathly quiet. My mouth was dry as paper. I could hardly swallow.

The voice of the NASA man, which had been incredibly calm throughout the countdown, moved up a register: 'Eleven, ten, nine ... ignition sequence starts ... six, five, four, three, two, one, zero ...'

I couldn't hold myself back any more. 'Go!' I roared at the screen.

Sean sprang from his chair. 'Go on! Go on!'

'Lift off ... we have a lift off!' the man from NASA confirmed as the flaming beast lumbered off Launch Pad 39A and slowly cleared the tower.

25

After all the hot, dizzy excitement I needed to get to the sea and cool down.

I had hoped Eilis would come to try out her new surfboard and talk about the fox, but her dad had asked her to help with the hay. So I strolled alone down the winding bohereen, listening to the chirping of birds and the hum of bees. Soon the sound of the waves rose up and I could smell the salty sea air.

I put on my swim fins and hit the water.

I went out beyond the breaking waves and swam parallel to the shore: a brisk one hundred strokes this way, toward Mount Brandon; another hundred strokes that way, towards the little line of hills called The Three Sisters. It's best to keep moving when the water's cold, so I decided to have a go at bodysurfing immediately.

Jimmy had told me to try bodysurfing with fins, the way they do it in those big waves in California. He'd said it was even better than surfing with a board. I was a confident swimmer and, with those fins on, I could move like a fish.

I built up some momentum and as the wave crested behind me I lunged towards the shore, all the time paddling furiously. What amazed me was that I was able to angle across the wave, something I couldn't do with my surfboard. In that moment I was at one with the wave, in the wave, the two of us charging together like buffalo in a stampede. But the best was to come. A second or two later, the crest caught up, the wave closed over and I was buried in its white foam and shot forward like a rocket. Now my body was the board, happy to go wherever the wave brought me. It brought me right on my belly onto the sand.

I was buzzing!

If I bodysurfed one wave, I must have bodysurfed twenty. With all the thrashing around in the water, I didn't feel the cold.

Afterwards, I ran to the end of the beach and back.

By now, Mom and Lucy had arrived down by car. My sister, of course, had not forgotten my promise about Daddy Moo-Moo and reminded me, over and over. To keep her happy, I brought her down to the rock pools. We clambered over the rocks in our bare feet, peering into every pool. Lucy had a bucket with her and we brought back a collection of pebbles, shells and two live crabs to Mom.

I wasn't done with the ocean, though. Mom and Lucy were going swimming – well, paddling, to be more accurate – and I decided to join them. This time I brought my mask with me.

Once more I went out beyond the waves. I flipped over for a lazy backstroke and then slowed until I lay there floating, motionless, with my head back in the water. I could hear my breathing. I stared up at the blue sky thinking of the three astronauts. Right now those men were orbiting the earth. If they looked out their window they'd see this ocean below them.

They're floating in air and I'm floating in this here water, I thought happily.

I pulled the mask down over my eyes and let myself sink.

Eyes closed, I twisted, turned and rolled over, feeling what it must be like to be a spaceman floating above the earth. Mr Walker says that those NASA astronauts spent a lot of time training in water tanks, and it was easy to see why.

I opened my eyes. I found myself looking through a crystal window to another dreamy world. All around, the marine blue was filled with light and, below me, the sand shimmered. All was clean, clear and bright.

Could space be this beautiful? I wondered.

Close by, a hundred or more tiny fish glided in a shoal. I tried to swim in pursuit but they gently veered away and disappeared into the shelving green-blue depths.

I came up and broke the surface, gasping for air.

Then I lay back and floated again. And as I did, the stuffed fox floated into my mind. Had I thought this thing through? Did I really think Grandpa would fall for it? Was he that stupid? And if he falls for it, what happens if the fox shows up at the hen house the following night? And what about the tail and the bounty?

The more I thought about it, the more it felt wrong. I loved my grandfather and I didn't want to make a fool of him. Or make myself look – as Eilis would say – like an eejit.

Maybe I should call the whole thing off? I thought.

26

Mom dropped me at the Bakers' on the way home from the beach. When Lucy realised I wasn't taking her with me, she went into orbit. She started to wail, the tears coursing down her red cheeks. I felt bad.

'I promise I'll bring you to Daddy Moo-Moo when I come back,' I said as I shut the car door. I turned to Mom. 'What's this thing about Daddy Moo-Moo anyways?' I asked, exasperated. But Mom just gave me one of her Danny-I'm-somewhat-disappointed-in-you looks. Which wasn't fair. Mom knew I had to deal with this fox business. I could get back to Lucy later. If she came now, Lucy would see what we were up to. Then the cat would really be out of the bag, so to speak.

I opened the trunk and took out the big brown bag. When I handed Mom back the keys, she drove off without any goodbye and I could hear my sister crying above the sound of the engine.

That fox has brought nothing but trouble, I said to myself.

The Bakers' rusty gate creaked as I went through, hoping nobody was listening or watching. I needed to hide the bag somewhere in the garden – fast. But I had to do it coolly, the way they do the drop-off in *Mission: Impossible*, making it look as if it was the most natural thing in the world to do, to put a million dollars under a restaurant table or drop a dead fox in somebody's garden.

I stashed the bag under a bush.

It took a couple of knocks before Sean opened the door. His freckled face beamed like sunshine. 'Is it yourself?'

'Yeah, it is,' I said. 'Is herself around?' I was even beginning to talk like the Irish.

'She's still at the hay,' he answered. 'And himself was here too.'

'Who's himself?'

He spelled it out for me. 'P-A-U-L!'

I shrugged my shoulders. I mean, who cares? 'Listen,' I said without a pause. 'I just need to see Eilis for a few moments.'

He waved his arm around like a propeller. 'Off you go so!'

'See you later then,' I said.

'Oh, and Danny?' he called after me.

I stopped and turned. 'Yeah?'

He gave a crafty wink of his eye. 'We're on your side!'

I shrugged my shoulders again, as if to say 'I don't know what you're talking about.'

The haymaking was in full swing. Eilis was there with her dad and Mike and Mike's buddy, Donal. They were making bigger haystacks out of the smaller ones they had made earlier. Eilis's dad was standing on top of one haystack and Mike was on top of the other. Eilis and Donal's job was to supply them with hay which they laid down in circular layers that decreased as you reached the top. A number of these seven-foot-tall haystacks were already made and, although there was little left to do, I figured I should lend a hand. I picked up a rake and began dragging loose bits of hay towards Donal's stack.

'Good man,' said Mr Baker. Eilis gave me the thumbs-up.

Then Mike said something in Irish (I think it was about me) and they all laughed except Eilis, who said something back to them. I think Mike had made some remark about that Paul guy and me, but Eilis wouldn't say when I asked her. 'Ah, nothing. They're just messing.' She smiled.

We worked side by side and I told her what I had hidden in the garden.

'Well, aren't you the proper little divil!' she laughed. 'I'll have to see this.' She stuck her pitchfork into the ground and declared loudly: 'We're taking a break, so we are. Come on, Danny.'

She strode off and I followed.

Eilis, like Mom, nearly went into hysterics when she saw my glassy-eyed fox peering out of the bag. I had to tell her to be quiet or Sean or someone would hear.

'How much did you pay for it?' she asked, clamping her hand over her mouth.

'Five pounds,' I replied.

She gasped. 'Five pounds? You're mad!'

'You're right,' I said. 'It won't work. I'll bring the fox back to the shop.'

'You will in your foot!' she exclaimed. She snatched the bag from me. 'Let's go.'

'Now, hold on here a second,' I called after her.

I followed her out of the garden, still protesting.

'You have to stick with the plan,' she replied over her shoulder. 'He'll be out with the gun this evening.'

I glanced at my watch. It was 6 p.m..

'He won't fall for it,' I insisted.

'Of course he will.' She stopped at the gate to the field and thrust the bag back in my arms. 'Here, pass this over to me.' She swung her legs over the gate.

'Look, that fox has caused him a lot of trouble,' I sighed.

'But she's beautiful.'

'Yeah, and so are my grandpa's chickens.'

Her eyes looked into mine. 'She's got to feed her babies, hasn't she?'

I shrugged again.

'Here, give me that.' She held out her hands and I passed the fox over the gate.

I climbed over and had to skip along to catch up with her. In seconds she was laughing again, giggling to herself. 'You're a gas man, Danny Sullivan.'

'When those foxes see this thing, they'll rip it to shreds,' I said gloomily.

She found this hilarious. 'Shut up, will you!' she cried.

When we approached the outcrop of rock, Eilis put a finger to her lips and we hunkered down in the long grass. We scanned the area for any sign of the fox family, like paw prints, poop or even feathers.

'We've got to think carefully about where to put it,' I said as I pulled my fox from the bag.

'Have you a name for him?' Eilis whispered. She was hugely enjoying all of this.

'Nope.'

'Let's call him Rowdy.'

'Well, I think we should put Rowdy high up on the rock there, where the foxes won't bother climbing up to him,' I said, 'and where Grandpa will just about be able to see and pop a shot at him.' Of course it was me – not Grandpa – who was going to get to climb up and deal with the, eh, body.

'Good plan, Batman,' said Eilis.

'The tail's the problem,' I sighed. I didn't know anything about stuffing animals but the tail would fool no-one. It was sticking straight out of the fox's body and was as hard as a poker. They must have put wire or wood or something inside it. 'How am I going to chop this thing off?' I said. 'If he gets to handle it, he'll know straight away.'

'We'll cross that bridge when we come to it,' said Eilis. 'Now, let's move.'

We made our way around the back of the outcrop, out of sight of the farmhouse. Wherever those foxes were, they were lying low.

Rowdy had been mounted on a flat piece of wood. I figured it was best to remove it. Fortunately, it came away easily.

Then we climbed the rock.

Poor old Rowdy. I wondered what had happened to him to end up like this? He was once a happy, carefree fox too, roaming the land, a-huntin' and a-rustlin'. But one day he'd been gunned down, or maybe he'd been hunted the way they do it in Ireland with horses and foxhounds ... Now he was about to be struck down again – by Grandpa.

I found a good place for him: on a ledge, looking out over the scene, but not too obvious. To tell the truth, when we got back down and gazed at ol' Rowdy up there surveying his kingdom like the Prince of Foxes, the set-up was perfect. Even I couldn't tell it wasn't a real fox, staring silently from its rocky throne.

'It's like something out of a movie set,' I said.

'If that doesn't fool him, nothing will,' said Eilis. She patted me on the shoulder. 'It's up to you now.'

'I'll do my best.' My neck felt tight, sore; I rubbed it. 'If he's going out with that gun this evening, I'll be with him.'

'I'll keep an eye out for you,' she said.

After that, we parted.

Dinner was ready when I arrived. Lamb stew, my favourite. I was starving and ate like a wolf.

I glanced at my sister. 'Are you not talking to me, Lucy?'

She gave me a hurt look, straight in the eye.

'I'm sorry,' I said. 'I promise, as soon as dinner is over, I'll bring you down to see Daddy Moo-Moo. Okay?' Her expression seemed uncertain, as if she didn't believe my promises any more. 'And we can stop off and say hello to Hello on the way if you want?' I added.

'That'll be fun, won't it, honey?' said Mom.

Lucy nodded but said nothing.

'Where's Grandpa, by the way?' I asked.

'Mommy, Danny's talking with his mouth full again,' Lucy spoke up, like she still hadn't forgiven me.

'He is too,' said Mom.

I made a funny face at Lucy.

'And what have you done with the you-know-what?' asked Mom.

'Nothing,' I responded. 'So where's Grandpa?'

'He went to the village about an hour ago,' said Mom.

'Has he had dinner yet?'

'No.'

There was still plenty of time to take Lucy down to the Bakers, so as soon as I had finished dinner, swallowed a cup of tea and munched some cookies we headed out the door.

'I love you, Danny,' she said simply, taking my hand as we strolled down the bohereen.

'You're the best in the west,' I replied.

The Bakers were still working away in the big field. The bull was in the field next to the house.

Despite calling out to him a number of times, he gave us the cold shoulder. It wasn't as if he was at the other end of the field either. He was close by, tearing up the grass with short concentrated bites. I was sure he glanced up at us at one point without raising his head, fixing us with his nasty eyes. I had no doubt he was the meanest son-of-a-gun.

Lucy stood on the stone wall, holding onto me with one hand, clutching a clump of grass with the other. 'Why won't Daddy Moo-Moo come?' she asked sadly.

'Don't know.' I sighed. 'I guess he just prefers his own company. But Hello comes, doesn't he?'

'Yes,' said Lucy, brightening. 'And he wags his tail.'

'Cool,' I said. 'We'll go see him next.'

When we finally made it back to the farmhouse, Grandpa was there with a friend of his, an old fellow called Charlie with twinkling eyes and a deeply lined face. Mom had served them dinner and now they were sipping some of that whiskey she had brought back from Tralee. Charlie had a bone-crusher of a handshake too and when he commanded me to 'pull up a chair', I knew we were settling in for the evening.

'Charlie's a character,' Mom whispered in my ear as she handed me and Lucy a glass of soda pop.

It was clear there would be no fox-shoot tonight. I was disappointed because I was keyed up for it and wanted to get the whole thing done and dusted.

After a while, I just sat back and listened. The men had one story after another: the fairies who lived on the back hill (Charlie swore he believed in them); the mean landlord who got what was coming to him; the big shipwreck; and the night of the great storm. Neither man mentioned the American astronauts who had blasted off for the moon just a few hours earlier.

Before I knew it, it was dark. Only then did I remember Rowdy, standing alone up there on top of his rock.

27

I woke up with Armstrong, Aldrin and Collins on my mind.

Yesterday, after orbiting earth a couple of times, they would have re-lit the third-stage rocket and struck out for the moon. It would take them four days to get there. I wondered what they were doing right now – like, what would they have for breakfast? What were they feeling as they peered out the window and saw their home, Planet Earth, now reduced to the size of a basketball, drifting further and further away from them.

Maybe they were too busy to look out that window. You could bet those bosses in NASA had worked out a pretty punishing schedule for them.

One thing for sure, if I were on board, schedule or no schedule, I'd be sitting by that window, staring out like a Zombie!

A rattle of cartwheels across the fields brought me back to earth.

It wasn't yet 8 a.m.. I could have some breakfast and still meet up with Eilis on her way to the creamery. She was always late, which was one reason she drove so wildly down the road. The other reason was that she was a bit crazy, but I liked that. I had never met a girl like that before.

I tiptoed down the stairs so as not to waken anyone. When I stepped into the kitchen, who was sitting there only Grandpa.

The gun was cradled in his lap.

'You're not going hunting, are you?' I gasped.

'I already have.' He kept wiping the wooden stock with a flannel, slowly, carefully.

'What? This morning?'

'At the crack of dawn.'

My heart was thumping. 'Any luck?' I managed to say.

'Not this time.'

I felt relieved but stood there saying nothing, waiting to hear what he would say next. Surely the game was up. He must have seen the stuffed fox. He's not blind; he couldn't have missed it.

'There's a pot of tay on the stove,' he said without looking up from his gun.

'Thanks,' I muttered. I poured the tea, cut a thick slice of bread and spread it with raspberry jelly. Then I remembered Mom had bought Cornflakes in Tralee, so I filled myself a bowl.

All the while, Grandpa sat there quietly polishing his gun.

Maybe he can't see too well, I thought. I figured everything must be okay.

'I guess you'll go hunting later on?' I ventured.

'I guess so,' he echoed, putting on an American accent.

'I'll join you,' I said with a big grin.

'You're welcome to, cowboy.'

I sat down with my bowl of cereal. 'So what do you think about those guys shooting off to the moon yesterday?'

'I remain sceptical.' The American accent was gone and he paused on the 'scep' bit.

'You wouldn't be if you watched it on television.'

'I don't need tell-e-vision to tell-e-me anything,' he snapped.

I was going to say something back but I held my tongue. Grandpa was just a bit grumpy after that whiskey last night.

Still, I wished I could convince him. As the man had said on TV yesterday: 'With this journey, man, who has lived all his life on earth, moves out into the solar system.'

In three hundred years' time, will anyone remember bands like the Beatles? Or even the Beach Boys? Or the boxing legend Muhammad Ali? Or President Nixon?

No, definitely not.

But they will remember the man who first steps onto the moon. I was sure of that.

Of course, that's if he ever gets to step on the moon in the first place, I thought as I cut down through the field to the road.

I climbed over the ditch onto the silent road and entered the bohereen on the other side. The rocky outcrop was just seventy yards away. I slunk towards it, peering through the brambles for any sign of Rowdy up there on his ledge. I couldn't see him, though.

Maybe he's fallen over? Or the foxes ambushed him? I thought. *Perhaps I need to get my eyes tested too.*

Suddenly I heard a noise from a low bush directly ahead. A fox scurried away. A second one followed. I think it was the mother and one of her cubs. Quick as a flash they were gone.

Since my cover was blown, I walked out into the open. I stood there, watching, listening. The only sound was the quiet *ticka-ticka-ticka* of a grasshopper. In the distance, a grey horse moved through the marshland close to the beach. I closed my eyes and felt the sun on my face.

I opened my eyes again and smiled. Those foxes were cool. They had a great life here. I was determined to save them – or at least to try.

I made my way towards the rock. There was no sign of ol' Rowdy. I was just about to climb up and investigate when I heard the mad rattle of cartwheels. Eilis was on her way.

I sprinted back to the road, getting there just as the horse and cart flew past. Eilis pulled up her horse and looked back over her shoulder at me.

I sprang on board. 'Rowdy's missing.'

She tapped her nose with her finger.

'So, it was you!' I gasped.

28

At least I'm going to get to the movie set today, I thought as we clattered back from the creamery on the Bakers' cart. *We might see some famous actors!* Eilis had the afternoon off and with the sun shining it was a perfect day for a long bike ride.

I raced up to get Grandpa's bike while she hurried off to get hers. Eilis had told me that Robert Mitchum was playing the part of a school teacher in *Ryan's Daughter* and that a beautiful actress was starring in the film too. As I ran up to the house I was really excited about the day we'd planned and spending it with Eilis.

The only problem was the bike wasn't there. Grandpa had gone to the village on it. I waited anxiously for him to come back, but he didn't show. Before long, Eilis cycled up the bohereen.

I explained the problem.

'That's okay,' she said, pointing towards the big pyramid-shaped mountain behind the farmhouse. 'Let's just walk to it up over the hill there.'

'Sure,' I said. I had wanted to climb that mountain anyway, just to get to the top and explore.

Grandpa's farm ran in a narrow strip from the sea right up the hillside, over a long, gently sloping ridge that looked down over the village. We followed a sheep track skirted by daisies and yellow gorse bushes, with the sun on our backs and small birds trilling above us. Every now and then you'd hear *snap!* Eilis told me it was the seed pods of the gorse bushes exploding.

'I bet my grandpa hates that sound. He doesn't like those

bushes,' I said, remembering how he'd hacked at them viciously with his axe.

We paused at the top of the ridge and looked down over the fields. You could just make out the white waves fringing the beach way off in the distance.

'Hey, there he is.' Eilis pointed out a figure on a bike leaving the village directly below us.

It was Grandpa all right – his erect posture and the slow, steady movement gave him away. Even if his house were on fire, my grandfather would stroll out the door.

'Remember to put Rowdy back on the rock this evening, won't you?' I said.

'Trust me,' said Eilis. 'I've everything under control.'

'Good, because believe me' – I pointed my hand like a pistol towards Grandpa – 'he'll be gunnin' for him tonight.'

When we came to the end of the ridge, the mountain rose steeply before us. We started to scramble up the rocks. Looking up at the huge peak, you thought it would take all day to climb but I was surprised at how quickly we progressed. I decided I wasn't going to look back over my shoulder until we reached the very top.

'You haven't told Sean about the fox, have you?' I asked, thinking about my hunting plans for the evening.

'No,' said Eilis. 'He's trying to nurse the kitten - it's sick.'

'What's up with it?'

'Don't know. Her eyes are all runny.'

'I had a hamster once,' I began. 'One morning I came down to breakfast, and it was lying in the cage instead of eating and chasing around. I gave him some water, and he drank it. I even took him out of the cage and put him in a special box with fur and cotton wool to keep him warm. We kept him like that for nearly three days …'

'Did he get better?'

'One morning I come down and he was all curled up like a little baby, fast asleep. And when I picked him up, he was really cold. And the thing is –' Suddenly I felt myself choking up. I gave a shrug and fell silent.

I felt weird, stupid. Why get upset about a hamster? Then I felt really bad, because I remembered when my father died I didn't cry, couldn't cry …

'Danny, are you okay?' I heard Eilis say.

'I'm good,' I said, looking intently at a bush.

We walked in silence for a while. It was best to stop talking anyway, because that mountain was getting steeper and steeper. Before long we were panting for air. Finally, we neared the top.

I turned to Eilis. 'Here's the thing about my hamster and your kitten,' I told her. 'The way I see it, they don't harm nobody. They're peaceful creatures. They mind their own business. They've as much right to be here as you or me or anyone else. Who's to say that we're any more important than they are? And I mean that!'

Eilis looked at me, surprised. Then, smiling, she held out her little finger. I stretched out my little finger and we linked.

'Up Kerry!' she said suddenly.

'The dog and the county!' I laughed. Then we hooted and cheered and ran the last few steps to the top of the pyramid mountain.

If I had been looking out the cockpit window of an airplane, the view could not have been better. I could see to the four corners of the earth!

Eilis proudly pointed out the landmarks, though I knew most of their names by now: Mount Brandon, the little mountain chain called the Three Sisters and the harbour in between. You could gaze at all of that and the sea beyond. Then turning anticlockwise, you saw a headland and the little cove nearby where my father used to swim; then some islands (Eilis said they were called the Blaskets), the nearest one just a mile or so off shore, resting in the blue waters like a giant whale.

Eilis turned, pointing out Mount Eagle behind us and the farms and fields of Dunquin. Her dad had told her that this whole stretch of land was barely six miles wide – like a finger pointing into the deep Atlantic towards America.

'I've never seen nothin' like this before,' I gasped. I loved Florida, but it was flat as a pancake. You could drive for miles and miles and you'd only see trees and swamp. OK, maybe a 'gator or two to make things interesting.

'Come on, we'll race to the village,' said Eilis.

'Where is it?' I said, scanning the hillside below.

But Eilis was gone.

I ran after her.

Ever tried to run down a mountain? Impossible. You can only run and bound down a mountain.

That's what we did. We went running and hollering, bounding like rabbits on the rough track. There were no rocks, though, just grass and heather. We went like the wind.

Here's another thing. It can take over an hour to climb a mountain but only five minutes to get down!

The movie set was on a plateau under the shoulder of the mountain, which was why I hadn't seen it from the top. They had built a village there of about twenty houses, stores and even a church, all overlooking the sea and the islands.

Eilis and I came tearing into the high street, like crazy cowboys.

The place was deserted. All you needed was a giant ball of tumbleweed blowing through and you'd have yourself a fine ghost town.

I always thought that in the movies – especially cowboy movies – they built only a cardboard cut-out of a town. Maybe they'd build an entire saloon and a sheriff's office, but the rest of the town would be fake – just fronts with doors and windows. But here they'd built an entire village.

We walked down the street, feeling a bit spooked.

'Mike got building work here over the winter,' said Eilis.

I walked over and smacked the wall of a house to test it. It was real, alright. I tried to open the door of a bar owned by one Thomas Ryan, but it was locked. We peered in through the window. You could see a few tables and chairs on a wooden floor, an old-style counter with two huge brass beer pumps and, behind it, some shelves with bottles of liquor.

However, across the street, the door to J.C. O'Callaghan's store wasn't locked. We stepped inside. It was an old-time general store, the shelves all packed with stuff. There were saddles and bridles hanging from the ceiling, the rich leather glistening in the light. There were trays of potatoes, bags of carrots, baskets of rock-hard bread, boxes of nails, tins of furniture polish, bottles of medicine – this shop sold everything. And there was candy in great glass jars. One of the jars was full of black-and-white-striped spheres the size of marbles.

'They're called Bulls'-eyes,' whispered Eilis.

'I like the name,' I said.

I couldn't resist the temptation. I went behind the counter, opened the lid and took a couple.

Eilis giggled and pointed a finger at me. 'You're bold!' But she didn't refuse when I offered her one.

We went outside and strolled on down the street.

'Hey, these Bulls'-eyes sure taste weird,' I said. The taste was strong and spicy.

'There's peppermint in them,' said Eilis.

It's funny the way they call candy *sweets* over here. A slice of bacon is a *rasher*. A lady bug is a *ladybird*. A trashcan is a *bin*. A drug store, a *chemist*. Weird.

We walked as far as the church at the end of the village and then turned back, still hoping we might see an actor.

'What'll happen to all this when the movie's over?' I wanted to know.

'Don't know, knock it down, I suppose,' said Eilis.

'Anyway, it looks like we won't get to meet Robert Mitchum today,' I said. 'Come on, I'll race you!'

I went off like a shot back up the village. Eilis came hot on my heels.

There was this big flat boulder lying at the side of the street. I came charging towards it, out of breath now, because we were running up a slope.

I made a great leap onto it ... and went crashing straight through.

The thing wasn't a boulder at all, at least not a real one. It was a prop made of fibreglass – paper-thin – and my two big feet went straight through it.

The look of shock on my face must have been something else. Eilis was in hysterics. I wanted to get out of there fast. I was really glad now that there was no-one around.

'Oh, we're going to be in trouble,' gasped Eilis, clamping her hand over her mouth as we hurried off. 'Aren't you some boyo, going around robbing and wrecking,' she said, elbowing me in the side. 'Sure, I can't bring you anywhere!'

'Don't tell anyone,' I said. I felt really bad about smashing the fake boulder, but how was I to know?

Instead of going back over the top of the mountain we trekked around the side and, after climbing over a pinnacle of rock, came down onto a steep road overlooking the sea. Below us to the right,

I saw the cove near my dad's old farmhouse, with large waves rolling in to the shore.

'Would you like to meet my dad's parents?' I asked.

She grinned. 'Sure, don't I know them well!'

I kept forgetting that everyone knew everybody else in this part of the world.

We didn't have to follow the road, as Eilis knew the way like the back of her hand. We cut down through the fields, making a beeline for the beach. As we walked, she gathered wildflowers growing in the meadows and on the ditches: poppies, daisies, buttercups and a lovely orange one. Normally I don't pick flowers, but seeing as it was for my grandma I helped her. Pretty soon we had gathered a fine bunch.

We climbed down through a gully where a stream ran off the mountainside, and stopped to scoop up the cold, refreshing water in our hands. Then we followed the rushing waters to where they spilled out over some dark rock and onto the golden sand of the beach.

Those waves were inviting and scary at the same time. There were some families on the beach with little kids pottering in the sand with their buckets and spades. A few brave parents stood in the water, letting it splash around their bare legs. One man charged into the thundering foam like a bull.

'So when will you come surfing?' I asked as we stared at the man, who began cutting through the waves with a vigorous stroke.

'And when are you getting up on my horse?' she challenged.

When we reached my grandparents' place, Eilis shoved the bunch of flowers into my hand. 'There you are now,' she said, knocking on the door.

There was a quiet shuffle of feet, then Grandma's smiling face appeared. The smell of freshly-baked scones filled the air …

29

The last thing I had said to Eilis when we parted was to make sure to put out the fox in good time. So where was it?

I stood in the meadow, a yard behind Grandpa, and stared up at the rock. It was dusk but you could still see quite well. Rowdy was not up there.

Grandpa was slightly stooped like a gunslinger, poised, his Winchester rifle held with both hands. Watching. Waiting.

It was so annoying. Everything had being going perfectly ...

When I had arrived back at the farmhouse, nobody was there. I was so tired from all that walking, I went upstairs to lie down. Somehow I fell asleep. It must have been a deep sleep too, because I didn't wake when Mom arrived back in the car. I was still dozing when I felt her hand shaking my shoulder. 'Dinner's ready,' she said quietly. I groaned and turned over.

Grandpa was in great form at dinner and chatted about the Bakers' hay and whether it would rain soon. We said nothing about shooting foxes.

I had a new, slightly different plan taking shape in my mind.

I washed the dishes, swept the floor, played with Lucy and generally hung about the place, all the time keeping a careful eye on Grandpa and the clock. Time passes slowly when you're waiting.

Finally, when Lucy's bedtime arrived and Mom brought her upstairs, Grandpa made his move (I think he might have been waiting till Lucy was off the scene). He'd been sitting in his chair by the window, eyes half-shut, doing nothing, saying very little.

'So,' he suddenly spoke up and rose to his feet. 'It's time to go.'

'I'm coming with you,' I said.

He paused and gave me that thoughtful look. 'Righty-o.'

While he went for his gun, I got myself a sharp kitchen knife, a paper bag and a spade. I waited for him outside in the yard. He came out the back door and around the side of the house. He stared at the implements I held.

'What have you got there?'

I brandished the knife. 'That's for the fox's tail,' I said.

'I thought that fox was a friend of yours?' The question was half-serious, half-joke.

I shrugged. 'It's for the bounty.'

That half-smile of his appeared again. 'I suppose you're going to smack him over the head with the spade, are you?'

'That's for burying the critter,' I replied. I was beginning to feel like I was in some kind of cowboy movie.

'Let's get on with it so,' he said, slinging his rifle back over his shoulder.

And here we were.

But where was Rowdy? I realised now that Eilis must have fallen asleep, as I had earlier.

Grandpa stepped out from the cover of the gorse bush and edged forward. The rifle was raised in his hands, though not in the firing position. Everything seemed to be deathly quiet.

He was just twenty yards away from the target area. I watched his head slowly turning as he scanned the terrain for his prey. I stood behind and stared, hoping the mother and her cubs would stay hidden.

A car passed on the road behind us. The noise of the engine ebbed away and silence returned. Those little midges that come out in Ireland at evening time were homing in on me, annoying me like hell.

All in an instant, Grandpa swung round to the rock with his rifle shoulder-high. In that second, I saw something move up on the rocks. It was the vixen!

The shot rang out. She fell backwards as if she'd been punched.

I felt sick.

Grandpa stood stone-still, rifle-at-the-ready, like a gunslinger waiting for the next move.

I was frozen for a moment. Then I managed to say, 'Wait, I'll go see.'

I clambered up over the rock with the knife in my hand.

To my utter amazement, Rowdy was lying there, shot. Right through the chest. His glass eye gleamed and he looked even more dead than before – if that was possible, considering he'd been stuffed in the first place.

Then Eilis's face peeked out at me from behind a slab of rock.

I must have had a really dumb – or dumbfounded – look on my face because she doubled over and clasped her mouth, trying to stop herself laughing.

'Well, what have you?' I heard my grandpa call from below.

I turned around to him and nearly lost my footing. 'It's a bullseye!' I shouted and no sooner had I uttered the words than I was laughing silently myself.

Have you ever been in a situation where you really shouldn't laugh but you can't stop? Like at school assembly when the principal is giving his talk. You're in the second row and the kid beside you says something stupid. You laugh, he snorts, then you both get hysterical. It's got to be one of the top ten awful-moments-to-be-stuck-in.

Well, I was stuck in it now.

Desperately trying to keep a straight face, I picked up Rowdy to show Grandpa. I lifted him as you would your own dog, with both hands under its belly, not the way you'd hold a smelly dead fox – by the tail or the leg. Rowdy's head was sticking up as if he was still alive, instead of lolling down. Realising my mistake I released my hold and grabbed the fox by the hind leg instead. 'Here he is,' I yelled, turning away quickly as more crazy laughter bubbled up inside me.

I fumbled with the knife. A few feet away, Eilis was leaning against a rock with tears of laughter rolling down her face.

I had to hack away at that tail about ten times before I succeeded in cutting it off. I held it up for my grandpa to see. I saw him nodding.

At this point my plan had been to pop the tail into the bag. The problem was, I'd left the bag on the ground next to the spade.

I felt myself sobering up as I clambered back down, clutching both knife and tail with the one hand. I prayed that he wouldn't ask me to hand it to him.

I tried to distract him by talking as I approached. 'Hey, that was a *great* shot. How did you do it? I never even saw it move up there. And you got it first time, clean shot, right through the heart. That fox didn't have a chance.'

He nodded to the tail. 'You'll have to bring that up to the guards.'

'I will,' I said. I picked up the bag and dropped the tail in. 'That fox won't be bothering your chickens again.'

'Where's the rest of it?'

'Don't worry about that,' I said. 'I'll look after that for you.' I brandished the spade to indicate my intentions.

He looked at me slightly quizzically. 'Very well,' he said. He stood there a moment, nodding to himself, as if surveying the situation. Then he slung the rifle over his shoulder and walked away.

30

I could have punched the air with happiness.

When Grandpa was out of sight, I made my way around the back of the outcrop. I whistled a couple of times and waited. Eilis did not appear.

'The coast is clear. You can come out now,' I hissed (not too loudly).

Still no response. I figured I'd climb up and investigate. I had one hand and one foot on the rock when she sprang out from behind and grabbed me round the waist. 'You're caught!' she yelled.

I almost jumped out of my skin.

The pair of us fell about the place laughing.

When I had recovered, I told her off. 'That was crazy what you did up there. You could have been killed.'

'*You're* crazy. It was your mad idea.'

'It wasn't my idea for you to be up there when he had the gun.'

'I wanted to make it look good. Your grandfather is not easily fooled, you know. Me and Rowdy had to work together on this one.' She sighed sadly. 'Poor old Rowdy.'

'Where is he?' I said. 'I'd better bury him.'

'You will not. I bags him.'

'What do you mean "bags him"?' I asked.

'Finders keepers!' she yelled and leapt up onto the rock.

I scrambled up after her.

No prizes for guessing who won.

'You can keep the tail,' she said to me, cradling Rowdy in her arms.

'Where are you going to keep him?'

'Well hidden,' she replied.

'Isn't he some sharpshooter,' I remarked, staring at the neat bullet-hole in our dummy fox.

Eilis nodded. 'He is that.'

I thought it was best to dig a messy hole, to make it look like I'd buried Rowdy. So I set to work. Somewhere nearby the real foxes were probably spying on us. I wondered what they made of all of this.

By the time we were done, night had fallen. I thanked her for her help and she thanked me for letting her keep Rowdy.

'I won't be around tomorrow,' Eilis said. 'My mother and I are off to Cork to visit my sister. We'll be staying overnight.'

'I'll see you Saturday then,' I said.

'Saturday so,' she answered jauntily. 'You'll be going to the *céilí*, won't you?'

'Guess so.' I smiled.

We said goodbye. She skipped away across the meadow with her prize tucked under her arm, and I headed homewards.

As I strolled back up the bohereen, I felt pleased with myself. Thanks to Eilis this had turned out much better than expected. I was 99 per cent sure we had fooled Grandpa.

31

Yet that 1 per cent of doubt lingered.

The next morning Grandpa was in the kitchen, shaving with the cut-throat razor. He glanced at me in the mirror when I sat at the table. 'So, did ye bury the fox?'

It wasn't so much the question that made me suspicious or the way he asked it. It was the 'ye' in it, because 'ye' over in this part of the world meant *you*, plural.

'Sure, yeah,' I fibbed.

That was all he said.

But that afternoon as I was about to head to the village to get some things in the shop for Mom, he stopped me on the bohereen. He looked at me, the bicycle and the shopping bag tied to the handlebars.

'Are you off to the village?' he asked.

'Yep.'

'Where's the fox tail?'

'My bedroom.'

'Go and fetch it.'

I looked at him, as if to say, *do I really have to?*

'Go on now,' he insisted.

I did as I was told. I think I knew what was happening, but he'd taken me by surprise and I'm not good at thinking on my feet.

I came back out of the house, tightly clutching the bag with the tail inside it.

'Take that tail – it's a brush, by the way – to the guards' barracks and collect the bounty. We'll split it fifty-fifty.'

I sensed that some kind of game of poker was being played.

'And how much will the bounty be, sir?' I asked, feeling suddenly nervous again.

'They'll tell you,' he said with a crafty glint in his eye. 'Now, off you go.'

What could I do? I cycled down the bohereen, ransacking my mind for the answer. I hadn't much time to think either because within five minutes I had arrived outside the police station in the village.

I couldn't go in. That would mean trying to get money under false pretences – from the police. They would never fall for Rowdy's tail anyway, once they picked it up and looked at it.

And I couldn't not go in. Where else, right now, was I going to get the bounty money?

I took the money Mom had given me out of my pocket and counted it. There was a red ten-shilling note and two of those massive half-crowns. That made fifteen shillings. But how much was that bounty? I took a deep breath and walked up the steps to the open door of the barracks.

A bare light-bulb hung over a table and chair in the office. There wasn't much else to see other than a few notices posted on the cream-coloured wall. After waiting a moment, I pressed the bell on the counter.

A well-built policeman with sandy hair and big red cheeks came into the room. 'What can I do for you?'

'I wanted to ask you a question, officer,' I began. As I spoke I noticed that my voice sounded nervous. 'How much is the fox bounty, sir?'

He gave an inquisitive smile. 'Are you John O'Shea's grandson?'

'I am.'

'From Chicago?'

I should have known. Things were getting complicated.

'We're living in Florida now, sir,' I replied.

'I see.' He leaned an elbow on the counter. 'And are you enjoying yourself in Kerry?'

'I'm having a great time.' I needed to get this conversation back on track and get out of there, fast. I cleared my throat and said, 'Officer, I was just passing by and I thought I'd drop in and ask you about the fox bounty.'

'The bounty. I see,' he said as if suddenly remembering. 'Have you shot a fox then? Is that why you're asking me?'

I gulped. 'Sort of, officer.'

'Sort of? What class of an answer is that?' He looked at me with a big good-humoured smile.

Was this guy playing poker with me too? Maybe he and Grandpa were in on this together? Or maybe I was beginning to get paranoid.

I just looked at him and grinned like a fool.

'So you shot Mister Fox did you?'

There was no way out of this one.

'I guess so,' I said.

'And you want to collect the bounty?'

I paused and thought, *Maybe I should just take the money from him?* Then I thought better of it.

'No, sir. I just want to know how much it is,' I answered him.

'You bring me the fox's tail and I'll give you ten shillings for it,' he said decisively. 'Would you be happy with that?'

'I would, officer.'

'Well and good so,' said the police officer.

'Thank you, officer,' I said and left.

Outside, I heaved a sigh of relief, worry and confusion all rolled into one.

I needed to get my head straight on this one – and fast.

Okay, Grandpa's waiting on a ten-shilling bounty and Mom's waiting on her shopping. I don't have enough money for both. That's one problem, I thought. *Also, that police officer knows Grandpa and is bound to tell him I called about the bounty but did not collect it. That's another problem … What am I going to do?*

There was one thing I could do. I went into the shop across the street.

The same lady was there, the one who adored Robert Mitchum. I explained that my mom had given me a list of things to buy but that I'd left some of the money behind and could I have some credit? She told me that was no problem. I thanked her and told her I'd come straight back with the rest of the money.

'And have you met Robert Mitchum yet?' she asked as I turned to go.

'No,' I replied. 'We went up to the movie set yesterday but no-one was there.'

'Well you should go up there today.'

I shrugged. 'Why?'

'Did you not see all the vehicles going up this morning?'

I shook my head.

'There was twenty or more of them, all passing by' – she swept her arm over the counter – 'trucks, vans, caravans, mini-buses and the swanky cars with the stars! They're filming today.'

'Maybe I'll go look for them,' I said, although I didn't really intend to. The *Apollo* astronauts were giving a live telecast later in the evening and I wanted to see it on the Bakers' television.

As I cycled homewards, I relaxed. There was no need to worry about that policeman talking to Grandpa. All I had to say was that I kept the tail because I wanted to. I could say I was going to give it to Grandpa as a gift.

Then I remembered what Mr Walker told us one day. 'A single lie can multiply.'

Mine was beginning to multiply. But there were good lies and bad lies, weren't there? Mr Walker had said so himself. In fact, sometimes to lie is the correct thing to do, he told us.

'Imagine, if you were going home from school one day and suddenly a terrified woman runs past you,' he said. 'The woman disappears around a corner. A moment later, a six-foot-tall madman with an axe appears. He roars at you: "Where did that woman go?" Should you tell the truth? Or tell a lie?'

Everyone agreed you should tell a lie. Except Jimmy Sunn. 'If you want to keep your head attached to your shoulders, sir, then I think you should tell the axe-man where the lady went,' said Jimmy.

The way he said it in that deadpan voice of his made us all laugh. Even Mr Walker smiled.

Grandpa was in the kitchen drinking tea with Mom when I breezed in. Lucy was sitting on a blanket on the floor with a red plastic tea-set that mom had bought her.

I slapped the ten-shilling note on the table. 'There's your fox bounty, sir,' I said.

Mom's eyes widened; she was trying not to smile.

'And here's your money, Mom,' I added, handing her a single half-crown.

'Why, thank you, Danny,' she said.

'You must have your share of it,' declared my grandfather, not looking up from his big mug of tea which he drank slowly and noisily.

'Nope.' I sounded emphatic. If Grandpa was playing poker, I had just whipped out a set of aces.

I put away the groceries (Mom is right: Grandpa really does need a refrigerator). Then I flew up the stairs to my bedroom. My money supplies were dwindling fast but I had enough to cover this venture. I grabbed a ten-shilling note, came back down and went straight out the door without saying anything. I jumped on the bike and rode back to the village.

When I arrived, the students from Dublin were hanging around outside the shop, eating ice-cream. Paul and Barry were there and the two girls, Rose and Joanna, were there too.

They – the girls, that is – smiled and said 'hi' as I went into the shop. I muttered 'hi' back.

As I got up on my bike to leave, Barry called me. 'Hey! Paul wants to know are you going to the *céilí* tomorrow?'

I turned. 'Why does he want to know that?'

'He's just interested, that's all!' The guy laughed and Paul shoved him away, laughing as well.

I shrugged to myself and said nothing.

'You better not dance with his girl!' Barry spluttered. He seemed to think he was hilariously funny.

'Don't worry, Danny. We'll dance with you! Won't we, Rose?' Joanna cut in.

The rest of the gang hooted and whistled. I smiled but felt myself blushing.

Later that evening, I went over to the Bakers and watched the telecast with Sean.

The three astronauts were now 100,000 miles from earth, winging their way to the lonesome moon. Neil Armstrong held a camera and did the filming as he and Buzz Aldrin climbed from *Columbia*, the command module, where they'd been since lift off, into *Eagle*, the lunar lander in which they hoped to descend to the moon's surface in two days' time.

Eagle was attached to *Columbia's* nose and you had to climb up through one and float down through the hatch in the ceiling into the other. I bet that felt weird for those astronauts, on top of everything else.

There were no shots out the window of earth falling away or the moon looming ahead or even the stars. It was amazing to watch, all the same, along with millions of others. Buzz Aldrin showed us the inside of the cabin and all the equipment in there – the flight plan, the visor he was going to wear when he walked on the moon, stuff like that.

The man on the TV invited us all to join him again tomorrow evening when, he said, *Apollo 11* would reach the moon.

I couldn't wait.

The only problem was the *céilí* would be on at the same time.

32

I went down to catch some waves on Saturday morning. It was my first visit since all the fox business.

There's something about the sea on a summer's day, the calm blueness, the wide-openness of water and the slow rhythm of the waves that makes you feel good. You're alone with the wind and the wave but you don't *feel* alone. You feel real – more real than you've ever felt. That wave bearing down on you will come once, and once only. Catch it and you're on a horse, galloping home.

Each day I was getting better at popping up and staying on my board. I was certain you could not angle across the wave with what I was using, but I was wrong. You can. Bodysurfing had taught me how to do it. You've just got to throw your body into it, in the direction you want to go, and the board will take you there – at least part of the way. I reckoned that if I had a proper surfboard, I could go all the way to surf heaven.

I decided that when I got home to Florida I'd save every cent and buy one. Then I'd head for Daytona.

Jimmy's dad learned to surf at the age of six. He said his people were surfing in Hawaii hundreds of years ago. Then one day the missionaries came. They told the people to stop surfing and it died away. 'We've an Irishman to thank for bring us back to it,' Mr Sunn once told me. 'Well, his father was Irish, anyways. His mom was Hawaiian.

'His name was George Freeth. He used to surf down at Waikiki where I hung out, but that was way before my time – I guess it was around 1910 or thereabouts. Now, there was a local boy by the name of Duke Kahanamoku, who went on to become an Olympic champion swimmer, and it was George who taught him how to surf. And Duke showed the rest of us. I remember when I was knee-high to a grasshopper seeing that guy surfing towards shore standing on his head!'

'That must've been something,' I said.

'It was.' He paused. 'As for George Freeth, he went to California and taught the folks there how to surf too. From there it spread across America ...'

As I walked back from the beach, I thought of George. Jimmy's dad had told me a lot more about him, about how he went on to become the world's first professional lifeguard, down at Venice Beach, and about how one day he singlehandedly saved the lives of eleven Japanese fishermen whose fishing boats were being swamped by huge waves. George dived in off the pier and swam out to them. He began guiding, pulling their boats, one after another, back towards the pier. A big crowd of people gathered to watch. For hours, George battled with the waves. Finally, after pulling yet another fisherman and boat to safety, he lay on the pier, exhausted, his body blue with the cold. There was still one boat out there. The people told him to leave it, that he wasn't up to it, that he'd drown if he went into the sea again. Against all the odds, George Freeth picked himself up and dived into the water one final time ...

The way Jimmy's dad told the tale, you expected to hear that George drowned that day. In fact, he rescued all of those eleven men and survived.

No wave could strike down this giant of a man. Instead a microscopic virus laid him low. In 1919, George Freeth died in the terrible flu epidemic that swept across the world at that time. He was thirty-five years old.

The same age my dad would be today, I thought.

But I didn't want to dwell on that. I switched my thoughts to the night ahead. I had a choice between going to a barn dance and watching *man reach the moon* on TV. Those astronauts were going to slot into the moon's orbit, zoom into and around the dark side and re-emerge, their cameras panning over the grey, pockmarked terrain seventy miles below.

How could I miss that?

Suddenly I thought of a solution. I'd persuade Eilis to stay at home for *Apollo 11*. We could go to the *céilí* next Saturday instead.

I called by the Baker place after supper, thinking I had given myself plenty of time, only to find that Eilis had already left for the *céilí*.

'She asked were you going,' said Sean.

'And what did you tell her?' I enquired.

'I said you were going, of course … You are, aren't you?'

I paused and said, 'Yep.'

If you can't beat 'em, join 'em, I thought.

I went home and put on a clean shirt.

33

When I came down to the kitchen, Mom was writing postcards, Lucy was playing with her doll Goldie, and Grandpa was drinking a huge mug of tea. I said my goodbyes, and slipped out.

Instead of taking the road to the village, I headed out the back way over the hill. Everything was quiet and still, with only the moths stirring. In the dusk, the darkness gathered on the land below, blurring the outline of fields and hedgerows, yet the sky above still glowed with a pale blue. Behind me on the left, a lone star shone high above the mountain ridge.

I thought about the fox and wondered what she was doing now. This was the time she went prowling. Would she dare to revisit my grandfather's hen house?

I should have checked it was locked before I left, I thought. *If the door's kept locked, there's no problem.*

Presently I came to the bohereen that ran down to the village. The faint sound of music drifted through the breathless air. I could feel my heart beating. I guess I was nervous.

There were a few cars and lots of bicycles outside the hall. Inside, it was full to bursting. I scanned the room and spotted Eilis and other familiar faces, like her brother Mike and the lady from the village shop.

The band was in full throttle on the stage: an old woman with a fiddle, a middle-aged man with a piano accordion and a kid with a tin whistle. They belted out their tune as the dancers skipped to the rhythm of the beat. The others, like me, clustered around the doorway or thereabouts, watching. You could tell the Dublin students, with their jeans and T-shirts, from the local guys who wore black trousers and white shirts rolled up at the sleeves.

The music stopped and the dancers cleared the floor, returning to chairs and benches on either side. I noticed that all the guys had moved to one side of the dance floor and all the girls to the other. While they were happy to dance, they weren't going to sit together and talk, or so it seemed. Only for that, I might have gone over and said 'hi' to Eilis; but I held back.

The man with the piano accordion, who was MC for the night, said something in Irish and next thing the floor filled again. Who did I see now but Paul, walking over and asking Eilis out to dance. She looked my way at that moment, but I pretended not to notice.

Joanna and Rose had also spotted me. They called me over and, to my horror, Joanna pulled me onto the dance floor.

All the dancers linked hands and formed up in lines of eight, each line facing the other a yard or two apart. I had Joanna on one side of me, Rose on the other. Our hands were held up at shoulder-level.

'It's called the Siege of Ennis,' said Rose, 'and it's dead-easy.'

I was not reassured.

Eilis was in a line with Paul and Barry some way up the hall.

The band started to play. With a skip and a step, each line of dancers advanced towards the other, retreated, then advanced and retreated once more.

'To the left now,' said Joanna as she and I skipped and swapped places in the line with Rose and her partner, another girl.

'To the right.' She steered me back again.

Suddenly Joanna let go of my hand. I wasn't left hanging, however, because the girl from the opposite line now took hold of me and we began to twirl round and around.

This was fun!

We broke off and joined ranks again. Once more the two lines advanced and retreated in time with the music. But as we came in the second time, all the dancers in the other line raised their arms and our line ducked under them.

Thus we moved to a new position facing a new line of dancers and started over. That's how this dance went, one wave of dancers sweeping through to meet the next, and so on, wave after wave.

Down the hall, I could see that Eilis, Barry and Paul were headed my way … and that Eilis would be right in line opposite me.

Although the windows were open, the heat was stifling. By the time they arrived, I was sweating.

As the two lines met, Eilis and I smiled a little uncomfortably. Paul pretended I wasn't there and I did likewise to him. But Barry gave me a friendly nod of the head and shouted, 'Up America!'

Then as Eilis and I came together to twirl she winked at me and said, 'Hi, stranger!'

And boy, did we spin. One was as crazy as the other. In that moment, I realised what it's like to be an astronaut in a centrifuge.

Before I knew it, the two lines had swept on past each other. I resolved to ask Eilis out for the next dance.

It wasn't going to be easy. When the music stopped, the girls retreated to their seats and the boys to theirs. I was happy to see that Paul, like the rest of them, didn't dare to cross the line either.

Yet the funny thing was Joanna and Rose had joined me in the crowd at my end. Looking around, I noticed some other boys and girls were standing here too, chatting in groups. I figured that the place where we stood was a kind of No Man's Land.

The questions from the two girls came like machine-gun fire. 'Do you like Elvis?'

'Have you ever been to Hollywood?'

'Have you got colour television?'

I did my best to answer whilst glancing up to see what Eilis was doing.

Before I knew it, the music started up again. The boys sprang from their seats like something out of that crazy film *The Invasion of the Body Snatchers*.

I didn't stand a chance.

Paul made a beeline towards Eilis but suddenly Barry overtook him – he actually broke into a run – and asked her to dance first. Paul had a look of thunder; his friend just grinned over his shoulder at him. That fellow Barry was a bit of a joker.

'This one is called the Walls of Limerick,' Rose told me. She elbowed her friend. 'I bags him this time!'

'Go on, you brat,' laughed Joanna. She turned and grabbed another girl behind her. 'Come on, Eileen!'

I was steered back onto the floor.

The music started up and away we went. This dance was similar to the last but with some variation; it went on for about ten to fifteen minutes. There was no air conditioning in the hall (unlike in Florida) and the heat was getting to me.

After that dance, I offered to buy Joanna and Rose a soda, or 'mineral' as they call them over here. There was already a line of thirsty people in the hallway looking to buy sodas and I didn't mind the wait, for the air was cooler out there. I handed a ten-shilling note to the man behind the hatch and, as I did so, the band launched into another tune, a slower one this time. The man gave me three bottles, three straws and a ton of change.

I went back inside.

The first thing I saw was Joanna and Rose out on the floor dancing to an old-time waltz. They both gave a little wave. Then

I saw Eilis and Paul hand in hand slowly circling the floor. I was the fool left standing with my three bottles and straws.

The waltz went on for ages. I felt a wave of disappointment. Not because I had missed the telecast, but because … I felt like a fish out of water, a 'right eejit' as Grandpa might say, and Eilis was dancing with someone else.

'How's it going?' A hand slapped me on the shoulder. It was Barry.

'Good,' I said, through gritted teeth.

'Don't you hate that Paul fellow?' he said.

I laughed quietly.

Barry offered me a chewing gum and I took it.

'Anyway, I'm off home,' he yawned. 'Good luck.'

'Thanks, I'll be seeing you,' I said.

I drank my soda and handed the two bottles to Joanna and Rose when they finished their dance. Then, making my excuses, I headed home myself.

34

Sunday 20 July 1969: now that's a day to remember.

I spent most of it hanging around the place doing nothing. I didn't call down to the Bakers' or go to the beach. As evening drew in, *the telecast of all telecasts* was about to begin and I was still wasting time. I was alone in the kitchen, reading the *Kerryman* newspaper, when I heard a knock on the door.

It was Eilis.

'Hello,' she said.

'Hi,' I replied.

'Where did you run off to last night?'

I shrugged. 'No place.'

The hint of the smile on her face vanished. 'What do you mean "no place"? You ran off early without saying goodbye.'

'I didn't "run off".'

'Where were you then?'

'Where were you?' I threw back at her.

'Dancing.'

'Exactly.'

She looked hurt. 'What's wrong with that?'

'There's nothing wrong with that.'

'You were dancing too – with those girls.'

'So what if I was? You were dancing with him.'

'Who?'

'You know. Paul.'

'You were dancing with Joanna.'

'So?'

'So? I was dancing with my brother as well, by the way.'

'And I was standing around watching most of the time.'

'You could have asked – you could have danced if you wanted to.'

I sighed. 'I can't dance anyway.'

'It's only a bit of fun.'

'Maybe,' I said.

'Anyway, I'm not interested in all that boyfriend business.'

'Me neither,' I agreed. 'I mean, in the girlfriend side of things.'

'It's silly,' she said.

'Too complicated,' I added.

'It's better to be just friends.'

'I agree. Totally.'

'Okay so.'

We said nothing for a little while, but that was cool.

'Righty-o, I'm off,' she sang out. 'Are you going to come down to see the boys land on the moon?'

I didn't need much persuading. 'Yep!' I said.

She smiled sweetly. 'See you in a while.'

'You sure will.'

She turned to go then paused and said, 'So, I'm not interested in Paul, in case you wanted to know.'

'Sure. And I'm not interested in Joanna either,' I said. 'Or Rose.'

She giggled. 'Or Barry.'

'I guess we're not interested in anybody.' I laughed.

'Sure aren't they leaving on Wednesday anyway?' she said.

'Is that so?' I said. (I was sounding more Irish by the day.) 'What a pity!' I said. We both laughed.

35

There are three of them. Slung out in the abyss of space. They'll have only one shot at this. They must be tired. They haven't slept much, or even washed, in four days.

Home is a dream away, a blue marble across an ocean of darkness. The moon, pale as death, looms up before them.

Collins stays on the ship called *Columbia*. He's flying that tin can round and round, hoping Aldrin and Armstrong will make it back sometime soon. A short while ago he wished them good luck as they climbed into that weird insect-shaped cabin, nicknamed *Eagle*.

Eagle's walls are as thin as the skin of a balloon. There are no seats. Surrounded by dials and switches, the two men are standing up before a set of hand controls at waist level. They peer out through two small triangular windows in front of them. The go-ahead comes from the NASA man over a quarter of a million miles away.

Aldrin presses the button. 'Ignition,' he says.

The Bakers' living room is packed with people. The lady from the village shop is there (her name is Lisa) with her husband and two kids. Other kids are sitting on the floor in front of the TV. Lucy's in the middle, sucking her thumb, staring intently at the screen. The older people are perched on the sofa and chairs, with others standing behind them and in the doorway. It's hot and airless, even though the windows are open.

The powered descent begins. It takes *Eagle* only thirty seconds to drop from seventy miles to just 50,000 feet above the moon.

A high-pitched alarm bell suddenly rings. 'Programme alarm,' warns Armstrong.

'We're "Go" on that alarm,' the voice from earth assures him.

At 7,500 feet, right on cue, *Eagle* pitches into a facedown position and the two men look down on the Sea of Tranquillity, which is pock-marked with craters.

Seconds later, they're at 3,000 feet coming down now at only fifty miles an hour. That alarm bell sounds again. 'Programme alarm,' warns Aldrin.

'We're "Go",' says the voice.

You could hear a pin drop in the room. Everyone stares at the TV as the moon's surface glides across the screen. The TV presenter is struck dumb too.

'Altitude 1600,' says Aldrin.

They're lower now than the height of the pyramid mountain behind Grandpa's farmhouse.

'Five hundred and forty feet,' says Aldrin, as cool as ice.

Suddenly the TV presenter finds his voice. 'According to the computer program, Armstrong contains the time of landing by taking over control,' he cuts in. 'Two hundred feet to go!'

They're really close now, but it's hard to tell from the TV picture because the grey surface of the moon is coming closer and closer but it doesn't have any real features, like mountains.

'One hundred feet,' says Aldrin. 'Forward, forward ... Thirty feet ... Picking up some dust ...'

Beneath *Eagle* you can see a jet of dust streaming away to the right.

'Forward, drifting to the right a little ... Contact light ... Okay, engine stopped,' Aldrin announces.

'They've landed!' Mom quietly gasps.

Armstrong speaks up for the first time. 'Houston, Tranquillity Base here. The *Eagle* has landed.'

'Roger, Tranquillity, we copy you on the ground,' says the voice from earth. 'You got a bunch of guys about to turn blue. We're breathing again …'

I felt myself breathing again too. All the people in the room stared at each other in wonder.

'They're on the moon, honey,' says Mom, picking Lucy up off the floor. 'The men are on the moon.'

I'm not sure my sister understood.

36

'The astronauts are going to walk on the moon,' I said to Mom, 'Grandpa's got to see this!'

'You won't persuade him,' said Mom.

'I will,' I replied.

The telecast had ended twenty minutes earlier; it would restart at 11.30 and remain on-air all night.

Nora Baker was serving cups of tea while Eilis and Sean passed around plates of sandwiches with thick orange cheese in them. A couple of men left to visit the bar in the village, promising to return for the scheduled moonwalk.

I grabbed a sandwich and slipped out the door. Earlier that evening I had seen the faint half-moon in the sky but as I walked up the bohereen there was no trace of it.

I approached the house and Kerry the dog trotted up to me, his tail wagging like crazy. The two of us went to check the hen house. I had been doing this nightly since the fox's last visit, just to be sure. There wasn't a sound or a stir from the chickens inside. They were either asleep or very spooked.

I'd hate to be a chicken, I thought to myself. *Their career prospects are not good!*

Grandpa was sitting in the dark – nodding off, I'm sure – when I came in. I didn't see him and switched on the light.

'It's yourself,' he announced, opening his eyes with a start.

'It sure is,' I said. 'Can I make you a cup of tea?'

'You're a good boy,' he said.

171

I took it that meant yes, so I filled the kettle with water.

'Will you come back down to the Bakers with me?' I asked.

'The Bakers? Why?'

'They're all watching the moon landing.'

'Oh, that.'

I paused, thinking of what to say next. 'Can I say something, Grandpa?' I began. 'I have this teacher, see, and he knows a lot of things. I mean, a *lot*.'

'He must be a good teacher so.'

'Remember when you were telling me about Charles Lindbergh? About how you saw his airplane that day with your own two eyes. Well, our teacher told us stuff about Charles Lindbergh you might like to hear.'

'I would of course.' Grandpa yawned and stretched out his arms.

'Okay.' I put the two cups on the table, pulled over a chair and sat on the edge of it. 'Did you know that Lindbergh was interested in rockets as well as airplanes? In fact, he gave money to a man called Robert Goddard to help him build the first liquid-fuel rocket. Now, that's the first thing, Grandpa. Charles Lindbergh believed in rocket science.'

My grandfather gave a single, serious nod of the head.

'You remember *Apollo 8* last Christmas? Our teacher told us that the day before the launch the astronauts had a visit from Mr Lindbergh. They had lunch together and he told them about how he flew the Atlantic that day. And they told him about how they were going to fly to the moon the following day.'

'Is that so?'

'Yes,' I said, feeling I was finally getting through to him. 'And I know Charles Lindbergh is a man you respect, right?'

'I do, of course.'

'So if someone like him believes in space exploration, then

maybe there's a chance, just a tiny chance, that what's happening up there –' I pointed towards where I thought the moon might be – 'right now, at this very moment, is really happening.'

'Lindbergh believes in it, you say?'

'Yes, he does.'

'Well, that's something to ponder,' said Grandpa. 'Now are you going to make me that cup of tay?'

You can lead a horse to water, but you can't make him drink, I thought to myself as I spooned three sugars into his cup.

A while later, Mom came in the door with Lucy asleep in her arms and brought her upstairs to bed. I put the kettle on again to make a fresh pot of tea.

'We may as well have a little listen so,' said Grandpa. He got to his feet and walked over to the radio. His big fingers fumbled with the dial and the big box began to crackle and buzz. As he searched without success for the station, the noise veered from high-pitched squeals to deep ear-splitting detonations of sound, as if some demonic leprechaun was inside it trying to break out with a jackhammer.

'Blast you!' my grandfather swore at it. There was a risk he might put his fist through the thing.

'Here, let me try,' I offered. I found the right station just as Mom came downstairs.

'I thought you were going to wake the dead,' she said. 'That thing is definitely on its last legs.'

She held up a paper bag. 'This is especially for you, Dad,' she said. 'From Nora Baker.' In the last couple of days I noticed she hadn't been calling him *John* any more.

Grandpa grinned when he saw the big slab of cake the bag contained. That man was as tough as nails but he had a sweet tooth, though he'd never think of buying cake or candy for himself.

With Lucy asleep upstairs, Mom said she wouldn't go back to the Bakers. 'I'll listen on the radio with your grandfather. You go on down; it's about to start,' she said.

After I handed her the cup of tea, I left.

I'm sure you've heard of Murphy's Law. *Whatever can go wrong, will go wrong*, it says. Well, there was consternation when I arrived at the Bakers.

Why? The television wouldn't work, that's why. The only television set in the entire village and it breaks down.

Ask Murphy about it.

Mike and his friend were trying to get the picture back. Mike shifted the 'rabbit ears' to and fro while the other guy messed around with the controls at the back of the set. They got nowhere.

All the people in the room sat or stood about, waiting tensely. I couldn't help thinking that if I were back in Florida I'd be sitting comfortably on the sofa in front of our state-of-the-art colour TV or even watching it from Cape Kennedy. Across the room, Eilis looked at me, smiled and shrugged her shoulders.

Finally, Sean flung his arms in the air and snapped, 'Are you going to fix it or not Mike?'

His older brother threw him a dark look. 'Do you want a clout, boy?'

Everyone seemed to find this very amusing. However, a moment later, when the TV emitted a short death-screech and the blizzard of lights on the screen disappeared into one intensely bright pinprick in the centre, the room filled with a groan of dismay. We sensed that all was lost.

I don't believe this, I just don't believe this, I thought.

Eilis's voice broke the silence. 'Right, lads,' she called out. 'I vote we go outside and light a big bonfire. A bonfire so big and fiery they'll even see it from the moon!'

'Good idea,' agreed Sean.

Most of the younger people immediately sprang to their feet and hurried out the door with her. As for me, I hung back, hoping a miracle would happen, that this TV would somehow come back to life. I'd been having a great time in Kerry up to now. I felt like putting a sledgehammer through that box.

This is Mom's fault, I thought. *Why did she have to come to Ireland? I can forget about my space project. I can forget about writing all that stuff, with the big build-up about the space race, Saturn V, Apollo this, Apollo that … Because when you'd come to the moment, the moment of all moments, when history was being made, what would you have to write? 'Well, actually, I didn't get to witness that moonwalk part – the part that the 500 million other people saw – because I was in Ireland at the time and there was only one TV set in town, a black-and-white one, and it went on the blink.'*

Yeah, sure.

Mike and his friend kept twiddling and fiddling with the dead TV.

'You're wasting your time, boys,' Lisa, the shop lady, said knowingly. 'The transformer's gone.'

'She's right, son,' said Mrs Baker. 'Sure, can't we listen to it on the radio?'

What good is a radio? I thought.

I felt a hand tugging at my sleeve. Eilis had come back. She said nothing, just beckoned me to go outside with her. I exhaled deeply and followed her.

Outside, stars twinkled in the midnight sky above the silhouetted mountains. All was quiet but for the excited cries of the bonfire crew.

'The last time we lit a bonfire was when Kerry won the All-Ireland Final,' Eilis told me.

'And we'll win it again this year,' yelped Sean.

'Up Kerry!' cried Mike, who had thrown in the towel and stepped out behind us. He cupped his hands around his mouth and shouted out for all to hear: 'Come on, lads, we'll build a bonfire so high they'll see it on the moon!'

Everyone cheered.

We all went gathering wood for the fire. Lots of it was lying about: twigs, a few tree branches and old planks. Two kids – I think they were on vacation in the area – disappeared down the field and returned with bundles of hay. I heard Mike whisper to them to put them back before his dad saw them. You don't burn a farmer's hay, kids.

Though I didn't feel like it, I joined in. I searched the yard for stuff to burn, then drifted over towards the bohereen. Suddenly I heard a loud snort from the field and knew that the bull was there, on the other side of the hedgerow. It freaked me, knowing it was there. I stood in the darkness, listening. I knew it was listening too.

I slipped away and returned to the yard where, by now, the bonfire was crackling and devouring old branches and chunky logs. Pat Baker had really got things rolling with a match and a couple of rags doused in paraffin. Very dangerous, I'm told.

Soon we had ourselves a roaring inferno! The yellow-green flames licked higher and higher, spread wider and wider until we all had to back off from them. Sparks shot into air like tiny firecrackers celebrating the great occasion.

Eilis and her brothers clapped hands and started up a song in Irish. I hummed along with them. People drifted out of the house and some passers-by joined us. Soon there were about thirty or forty people there.

Later, an old man stopped by with a fiddle, probably on his way back from the pub. When he started to play, the dancing began. Everyone linked hands and stepped *1, 2, 3* and *1, 2, 3* in

176

a wide circle around our beacon fire. Around and around we went, the fiddle player grinning in a crazy, toothless way.

As I circled the flames I gazed into the starry sky and thought of Armstrong, Aldrin and Collins.

And the rest, as they say, is history.

37

After being up most of the night, I slept all day. It was not until the following day that Eilis and I finally met for our Great Surfing and Horseback Riding Challenge.

It hadn't gone well with her horse on the previous occasion, but that wasn't Lir's fault. This time I climbed into the saddle without mishap. Taking Lir by the reins, Eilis walked us down through the meadow towards the beach. Normally it was marshy and impassable, but dry weather had stiffened the soil.

As we neared the beach, swallows whizzed low over the grass, like fighter aircraft, banking this way and that, looping-the-loops and criss-crossing each other. Lir took no notice. For once, he seemed as steady as a rock. We climbed over a small sand dune and walked towards the shoreline.

'You've got an audience,' said Eilis.

Two hundred yards away, I saw Mom and Nora Baker, Lucy and Sean sitting together. Since we had arrived in Kerry, Mom had been trying to persuade Nora to take time out and join us for a picnic, and she had finally succeeded.

'Grip with your knees and hold the reins tight,' Eilis advised. 'And when you want him to move faster, kick with your heels, don't flap the reins.'

She stepped back and left it to me and Lir.

I'd love to say that I galloped, cantered or even trotted up that beach. I think *shuffled* would be the correct assessment.

'Go on, dig your heels in, Danny,' Eilis urged.

I did as I was told and got a bit of a response.

'If you feel yourself falling off, just grab his mane,' Eilis called after me.

Mom and Nora clapped their hands. Lucy gave her little wave.

'Come on, lift those legs!' Sean shouted out.

Lir slowed to a walk again after a few seconds and, since I wasn't going to argue with that, we ambled along the beach, taking life easy. It was my first time riding a horse and I didn't feel like playing the hero. In the same way that I feared the bull, I didn't trust this horse. The thing is, with a horse you never know when some freak accident might happen. A bee might sting him on the nose and send him crazy. I'd seen a horse getting spooked in Chicago once. Dad and Mom had brought me to a horse show; I was aged about five. Some of the kids were dressed in cowboy outfits, with guns and holsters, and at some point there was a competition for The Fastest Draw in the West. Two kids lined up facing each other about ten yards apart and when the judge dropped a white handkerchief they had to draw and shoot.

In the middle of all this, a woman shrieked.

Then I saw this crazy horse. It had just bolted, cut loose. People were running trying to get out of its way. The horse stampeded through the field, among the cars and tents.

It suddenly turned and came for us. Mom screamed. Dad scooped me up in his arms ...

No, I don't really trust horses.

I did trust waves, though. When it came to 'white horses', what you see is what you get.

After me and old Lir finally managed a U-turn at the end of the beach and had made our way back, Eilis was waiting in her blue swimming costume.

'So, where's my surfboard then?' She smiled.

'You can barely swim, girl – you're not to go out far,' her mother warned her.

I climbed down off the horse. 'You can't swim?'

'Of course I can. Don't mind my mother.' Eilis Baker was scared of nothing.

'Take it easy out there, Danny,' said Mom, giving me one of her looks.

I shrugged. 'Sure, I will.'

Eilis led the horse away to graze while I dragged the surfboards down from the dunes.

'For today, just stay in the white water and practise trying to get up on the board,' I cautioned. Laying the boards on the sand, I went through it all step-by-step: how to lie on the board; how to paddle; how to pop up and how to use your body to keep your balance.

'Have you got that?' I asked her.

'Ready when you are,' she replied.

Without further ado, we went down to the water.

The waves were just right, not too big, not too small. We strode waist-deep into the water. 'Just stay here and practise your technique,' I shouted above the roar of the broken waves. I pushed on ahead to get to where the real action was.

But do you think that girl listened to me? She came right behind me, pushing the board in front of her.

'Hold on there,' I shouted over my shoulder.

'I'm going to give it a shot,' she answered.

I felt uneasy, and I noticed her mother had stood up and was watching us intently.

I figured it was best to go first and give a demonstration so I got up on the board and paddled into a turn. As the wave nosed in, I caught it smoothly and sprang to my feet. Geronimo!

Whipping towards shore, I saw Mom and Mrs Baker walking to the water's edge. I jumped off my board and turned around. By now, Eilis was up to her shoulders in the water.

'Come in!' I heard her mother call. But Eilis couldn't hear.

'Bring her in, Danny!' Mom sounded anxious.

I let go of my board and ploughed through the water towards her. There was nothing I could do about it, however, because Eilis was going to have a shot and that was that.

I stopped swimming then and stared.

Still standing in the water, she had turned and pointed her board towards shore. At the last second, as the wave bore down on her, she pulled herself onto it and in one movement leapt up like a ballerina. Away she went on the crest of the wave. I had to dive to get out of her way.

It was hard to believe. On her very first try, that girl sailed through air and water like a goddess. Five seconds later she lost her balance and tipped over, but that's not the point.

I was stunned. 'You've done this before, haven't you?' I said when I caught up with her.

'That was fantastic!' she yelled.

Eilis was hooked.

I waved a finger at her. 'That's it now. Your mom looks a bit freaked.

'I'm doing it again,' she said. Eilis waved to her mother and turned back into the waves. Her mother shook her head and said something to Mom.

For the record, Eilis took three more tries but failed to ride a wave again.

We left the boards on the beach then and for another twenty minutes ducked, dived and bodysurfed in the white water. Eventually, the cold drove us from the sea.

The two moms were relaxed now, plying us with sandwiches and Mrs Baker's delicious scones – all washed down by hot tea from an ancient Thermos flask.

After that, Eilis took Lucy off to say hello to Lir, while I turned to the newspaper from the day before. TWO MEN WALK ON THE MOON ran the banner headline. 'One small step for man. One giant leap for mankind.' ARMSTRONG PILOTS *EAGLE* MANUALLY IN LAST STAGES OF LUNAR DESCENT.

It's not a great idea to read newspapers on a windy beach. Within seconds I was chasing pages all over the sand, much to my little sister's amusement. Which was a bit annoying, as I needed them for my space project …

38

The wind gathered in strength and by nightfall battalions of cloud and rain swept in from the Atlantic. The following morning mist had descended on the pyramid mountain and, across the bay, Mount Brandon was lost from view.

Standing in the doorway, I looked down to the shore and saw the white explosions of spray dashing onto the meadows. *Behind every cloud is a silver lining*, I thought, dying to get out with my board.

Mom must have been reading my mind. 'You can forget about surfing today, sonny. We're all off to Killarney.'

'No way! What for?'

'Your grandfather's refrigerator, that's what for,' she whispered. 'It's meant to be a surprise.'

'I don't need to come.'

'Yes, you do. I need your help with Lucy. Besides, Killarney is the prettiest place in Ireland and I'd like you to see it.'

I gestured to the rain and to the sheet of lead that was the sky. 'In this?'

'It can be raining here and sunny the other side of the mountain,' she said. 'Believe me, I know. I grew up here.'

For the record, it wasn't sunny on the other side of the mountain.

'The rain will have stopped by the time we get to Killarney,' said Mom, driving happily onwards.

It took another hour to get there.

'The rain's stopped, what did I tell you?' Mom parked the car and turned around, smiling at me. 'So am I right? Or am I right?'

I got out of the car and looked around. 'You're wrong, Mom. It's still raining,' I said.

'That's just a fine mist.' She laughed.

'It's called rain, Mom.'

'No, it's a soft Irish day, that's what it is,' said Mom. 'Now let's do some shopping.'

'Yes, Danny, we're doing shopping,' Lucy hissed at me.

'It *is* a pity, though. You should be able to see magnificent mountains from here,' groaned Mom.

I followed the pair of them along the busy street. Fortunately, there was only one electrical store in Killarney, with the same refrigerator models we'd seen in Tralee. Mom quickly chose one; and it didn't take long to buy the radio either.

Then we looked in a couple of shops for gifts to bring back to America. I bought a mug for Jimmy with heaps of shamrocks on it and the words *Céad Míle Failte*. Mom said the words mean *A Hundred Thousand Welcomes* and that is what everybody gets when they come to Ireland.

After lunch we took a ride in a horse and buggy, which they called a 'jaunting car'. We drove down by a lake near a big fancy house.

'Only for that mist, you'd have such a fantastic view from here,' said Mom again.

'I've heard that before,' I said.

Mom wasn't done yet. She drove us to Torc Waterfall, a few miles out of town. It wasn't Niagara Falls, but it was worth seeing.

Next stop was Lady's View, which was supposed to have an amazing view as well. *Supposed* - if you could have seen it. As we stared into the pillar of mist, Mom gave her running commentary. 'There are beautiful lakes and a river down there, set among ancient oak woodlands, all overlooked by majestic mountains,' she sighed. 'It's like something out of a Turner watercolour. He was a famous English artist, Danny.'

I shook my head. 'I'll take your word for it.'

By now, Lucy was cutting up and who could blame her? Mom bought her a big ice-cream cone which melted all over her hands and splattered her face. I had one as well. Mom had coffee, black and steaming hot.

As soon as we hit the road, Lucy fell asleep.

'So how's your moon project coming along then?' asked Mom as we hit the coast road again.

'I haven't done much.'

'Will you get in trouble with Mr Walker?'

'It's voluntary. It's not like it's an assignment or anything.'

'Sure,' said Mom. 'He's a nice person, isn't he? You like him?'

I shrugged. 'Yeah.'

'Well, there's something I've been meaning to tell you, Danny.'

We exchanged glances.

'You remember when Mr Walker dropped by,' she went on, 'the day before we left for Ireland?'

'Sure.'

'You had forgotten some books and stuff.'

'My NASA booklets.'

'That's right,' she said. She paused. 'Well, when he came over, he invited me out to a concert.'

'He asked you?'

'Yes.'

'He asked you out?'

'Yes, to the concert.'

'Like, on a date?'

'It's not a date. It's a concert. A Vivaldi concert.'

I was speechless.

'Vivaldi? Who are they? Some band or something?' I said finally.

'Vivaldi was a great Italian composer, Danny,' Mom said patiently. 'We're going to hear a chamber orchestra play his music.'

'So you're going?'

'I've given it some thought … and, yes, I've decided I'd like to go. It's in the town hall, this day week, at lunchtime.'

I looked away, out the window. The rain was starting up again.

'He's a nice man, Danny.'

'So what?'

'There's nothing for you to worry about.'

'I'm not worried,' I said. 'And I don't want to talk about it any more.'

'No problem,' said Mom.

We drove on for miles, listening to the beat of the windshield wipers.

'Hey, I've been meaning to tell you,' she said, suddenly breaking the silence. 'I met my cousin Sarah yesterday. She's got a job on the movie set – with your Robert Mitchum.'

I said nothing.

'She says there was a party in his house on Saturday night and one of the locals came up and punched him in the eye.'

'What for?'

'For no reason at all, Sarah says,' said Mom. 'The fellow just wanted to punch a famous movie star, that's all, and boast about it afterwards – you know the way Mitchum is supposed to be a tough guy and all that.'

'And what did Mitchum do about it?'

'I don't know. But they'll have to postpone the shoot till his eye gets better … And the thing is, he's not a tough guy at all, she says. Anybody who's met him here says he's the kindest, gentlest man you could ever meet.'

Hearing this upset me even more. 'I thought Ireland was supposed to be the land of the hundred thousand welcomes,' I said. 'You know, like it says on this here mug.'

Lucy must have woken up because just then she squeaked, 'Mommy, the moon is following us.'

Looking out, I saw the moon shining through a window in the clouds. 'It's going to race us all the way home,' I replied.

I thought of Eilis then and wondered whether she might come surfing when I got back. 'I've still time to catch some waves today,' I remarked.

'Maybe, but don't bring Eilis,' answered my mind-reading mother. 'You might be able to handle it, but it's too wild today for her. Her mom won't let her go.'

'But her Mom lets her ride that crazy horse and cart every day,' I said. 'They fly down the road at a hundred miles an hour.'

'Maybe, but that's a job for Eilis,' said Mom. 'The milk has to get to the creamery. To be honest, I'd prefer if you didn't surf today either. It's too rough. Imagine if you got hit by the board again.'

I decided not to argue the point. 'Maybe I'll bodysurf then,' I said.

'Maybe,' said Mom.

39

The astronauts were on their way home and I bet they were glad. The moon was a dead place. You'd never want to live there and you'd have no regrets leaving. You'd leave nothing and no-one behind. You'd never want to return.

In a couple of days, I'd be flying home too.

I wanted to go home, of course … and yet, somehow, I didn't – at least part of me didn't. I knew we wouldn't be back in a long time. Mom said as much herself, since it had cost a whole lot of dollars to get here.

I watched my grandfather in the kitchen and wondered when I would see him again, if ever. I thought of my other grandparents and felt bad that I hadn't been to visit them more.

Most of all I thought about Eilis.

But it wasn't so much what I thought of all these things as what I felt. And I just didn't feel good, yet I couldn't quite put my finger on it.

I was nursing a bad cold, which didn't help either.

'You're very quiet, Danny. Is everything okay?' Mom asked.

'Sure,' I said. 'I've just got a bit of a headache, that's all.'

The weather was cooler now, windy, with squally showers sweeping in off the ocean.

On Thursday, the TV repair man came over from Tralee. That evening we piled into the Bakers' sitting room and watched as Armstrong, Aldrin and Collins splashed down and were flown by helicopter to the deck of the aircraft carrier *Hornet*. Straight away, the three men were put into quarantine, locked away for weeks just in case they had brought back some bad moon germs.

Afterwards, walking home, I saw the full moon, with the clouds racing by, and heard the roar of the waves away down on the shore, like they were calling me.

40

The following morning I caught my final ride to the creamery. It was as scary as ever but great fun.

'I'm going to miss this,' I told Eilis on the way back.

'I've another idea,' she said, with a twinkle in her brown eyes. 'I've to go to the beach for some sand. We could do a bit of surfing if you like?'

I had to think before answering. 'It's wild out there right now. Maybe later,' I said.

'Come on, Danny, it'll be fun.' This girl was a daredevil through and through.

'I don't think your mom wants you to go,' I said.

'Don't mind her. Will we go down later?'

Again I had to think this one over. 'Maybe,' I said.

'All right, I'll leave off getting the sand till then.'

'Okay, but the wind will have to have died down,' I said.

She looked at me and frowned. 'Are you a man or a mouse?'

'Definitely a mouse,' I replied. 'And you're one crazy girl!'

I left her and went home feeling uneasy about the whole thing. Sure, I wanted to go surfing but I didn't want to worry about Eilis out there at the same time. *That's just too much to handle*, I thought. Besides, I had a bad feeling about it all. There were the two moms to contend with. If I sneaked down to the beach for some surfing with Eilis I could get in a lot of trouble.

So I hung around helping Grandpa on the farm all morning. The wind died down but the waves did not. After lunch, I stood outside the door and watched the spray erupt over the seaside fields.

Grandpa came out and stood beside me. 'It's the full moon that's the cause of those waves,' he remarked.

I didn't know what to do about Eilis.

When Lucy began pestering me to bring her down to the Bakers, I quickly agreed. 'Okay, come on,' I said. *Having to mind my sister is a good excuse not to go surfing,* I thought.

If she was disappointed, Eilis didn't let on. 'No bother, the three of us can just go and get some sand,' she said. 'Maybe we can surf in the evening?'

'Maybe,' I said.

Then Sean appeared. 'Let's play games,' he said.

'Hide-and-go-seek,' Lucy said.

'No. *Mission: Impossible,*' said Sean.

Lucy made a face.

'Please!' begged Sean. 'You're going back to America and we'll never get to play it again.'

'I want hide-and-go-seek,' my sister demanded.

'Lucy, *Mission: Impossible* is hide-and-go-seek,' I assured her.

She wasn't impressed. 'Don't want mission 'possible,' she said. But this time she didn't get her own way. We set up the game as Sean and Eilis on the IMF team tracking down Lucy and me, the dastardly duo.

When I tried to take Lucy by the hand to hide, she shooed me away. 'Don't want to!' she pouted.

'Okay, stay behind then,' I said.

Instead of heading off down the bohereen, as I knew they expected me to, I climbed in through the back of the barn. I tiptoed past Lir's empty stall, got down behind some bales of hay and waited. I chuckled to myself as I heard them calling each other outside, running this way and that.

Soon everything went quiet. They had obviously headed down the bohereen on a wild goose chase. Presently I heard their voices again.

'Check the garden,' I heard Sean say.

When the sound of his footsteps faded away, I crept out. I made my way to the side of the house and peeped around the corner. Sean and his sister were searching bushes by the front gate. I yelled at the top of my voice and scurried away. I planned to dive for cover inside the barn again, but as I ran for the entrance Sean ambushed me.

'Bang, bang, you're dead,' he roared.

I doubled up, fell on the ground and played dead.

Eilis ran up.

'Up you get, Danny,' said Sean. 'Let's play another game.'

'We'll do hide-and-go-seek for Lucy,' said Eilis. 'Where is she?'

I picked myself up and dusted myself down. There was no sign of my sister in the yard. 'She always does this,' I sighed.

Then Eilis's expression froze. As I turned to see what was wrong I heard her strangled whisper, 'Oh no.' But I still couldn't make out what was going on. Suddenly she sprang forward, almost knocking me out of the way. 'Lucy, come back!' she shrieked.

I turned and saw my little sister in her yellow summer dress standing in the middle of the field with her thin arms by her side. She held a clump of hay in her hand. In the corner of the field stood the bull, staring at her.

My mouth went dry and I felt weak, like I needed to sit down. It was that same feeling I'd had four years earlier when I awoke one November morning to find my dad's sister in our living room ...

By now, Eilis was up on the wall, waving her arms madly in the air, yelling, 'Lucy, Lucy, we've a game, come on, hurry, hurry!' The bull grunted and chucked his head up and down.

My sister slowly sat herself down on the grass, all the time looking at the bull.

I heard Eilis cry, 'Oh, my God, no!'

All I could do was stare as my sister lay flat on her back, pretending to play dead and finally catch Daddy Moo-Moo's attention once and for all. And, for sure, she had his attention. The beast stared back menacingly.

Then I heard someone yell from the other side, over by the bohereen. It was Pat Baker coming up the track with the horse and cart. In an instant, he jumped from the cart, vaulted over the low stone wall and sprinted towards Lucy. Injected with a sudden rage, the bull ran too. Or rather, he charged, head lowered, slow at first but quickly gathering to a thunderous pace.

In one movement, with one hand, Eilis's dad snatched my sister up off the ground. He raced towards us now, dragging Lucy like a lifeless rag doll under his arm.

Though the mindless bull rapidly bore down on him, I thought he was going to make it. And he would have too, if he hadn't had to get himself and Lucy over the stone wall, which was chest-high.

Pat Baker did what he had to do. Like an Olympic shot-putter, he hurled my sister into the air to safety, as he himself went down under the bull.

Eilis screamed. 'Daddy!'

I turned and saw my sister move, trying to push herself up off the soft grass where she had landed with such force. There was not a sound out of her. A few feet away, Sean whimpered. I turned back to the field and could not believe what I was seeing.

Pat Baker was back up on his feet and wrestling with the bull. Somehow he had managed to grab hold of the ring in the bull's snout. With both hands, with all his strength, with his feet pillared into the earth, he pulled on the ring, fighting to prevent the beast from lowering his massive head again. The bull snorted in fury and pushed the farmer back. I saw Pat's boots tear into the ground and heard him groan in desperate resistance.

At last I knew what to do. I dashed into the barn and grabbed a pitchfork. I ran back, intending to get up on the wall and hit the bull with it. But the battle had moved away from the wall and into the field. All the time, foot by foot, Pat was being pushed back, yet somehow he still managed to force the bull's head up to keep it from goring him.

Without a word, Eilis snatched the pitchfork from my hands. Then she leapt into the field and advanced towards the bull. Her father must have seen her for he roared out something in Irish and she backed away. She climbed back over the gate.

'What'll we do? What will we do?' she screamed over and over, tearing at her hair.

Lucy sat on the grass, sobbing and shaking. Sean raced towards the house to look for Mike or his mother, anyone to come and help. I ran too, out through the yard and onto the road to see if I could wave down a passing car or spot someone walking by. To no avail – the road was deserted.

Suddenly I had an idea. I ran back into the yard and grabbed the pitchfork again. 'Eilis, get the horse and cart!' I shouted.

We sprinted down the bohereen. Lir was waiting patiently, head bowed. Eilis leapt onto the cart and snatched up the reins. The horse was already moving by the time I scrambled up.

Sean pulled open the gate and we swung into the field.

Out there in the middle, Pat Baker was battling for his life. He still gripped the ring, pulling on it with all his might. The bull swung its head one way, then the other, yet the man lost neither his grip nor his balance.

Eilis stood up like a charioteer, while I hunkered down, tightly gripping the pitchfork. She clucked quietly to Lir and we took off. I expected her to make a beeline towards her father. Instead, she sped away down the side of the field. Approaching the end, she brought her horse into a wide turn.

'Go, boy, go!' she cried.

We thundered up the centre of the field. I should have felt scared but I didn't. I felt angry, mad angry. This beast had tried to kill my sister. Now it had attacked the man who had saved her life. I steadied myself and raised the pitchfork like a spear.

But there was no need for it.

Suddenly Pat sprang away from the bull and dashed towards us. As we flew by, he dived into the back of the cart. He rolled over on his back and cheered. I cheered too, and so did Eilis, all of us hollering as we raced for the open gate.

I looked back at the bull. He raised his head in the air and bellowed loudly. He did not pursue us, though. Instead, he turned and charged off down the field, his hooves ripping up the grass.

Once we got to the yard, I went straight to Lucy and took her up in my arms. 'You big silly billy,' I said stroking her hair. 'You silly billy.'

Afterwards, when our two moms arrived, there was a big scene. Pat had cuts and bruises but would not listen to his wife's advice to go to the doctor. He just smiled with a faraway look in his eyes. 'Sure, I'm as right as rain,' he kept saying.

Lucy had escaped without a scratch. She sat in Mom's lap sucking her thumb, and if Mom hugged her once, she hugged her a thousand times.

After things settled down, tea was made and Nora brought out her scones and everyone sat around talking about it all. Pat slapped me on the shoulder and said that it was my quick thinking that had saved the day.

'He's a great boy,' said Mom, looking proud.

I should have felt pleased. I should have felt happy.

But I felt bad.

After a while, I slipped out the door.

41

I packed my swim shorts and fins, took my grandfather's bicycle and took off down the road. I pedalled like someone in an old black-and-white movie trying to make a get-away. I didn't look up as I passed through the village.

My thoughts raced with me. *Why were they slapping me on the back? The whole thing was my fault in the first place. If I'd been minding my sister like I was supposed to, none of this would have happened.*

But it was more than that. A lot more. I had nearly lost my little sister. She had come that close. The image of her in the field with the bull repeated in my head. *Why was I so slow to react? What had I done for her?*

Then another picture welled up: my father, dark-haired and strong, like Pat Baker. I thought of him and pedalled furiously.

It was at the time when President Kennedy had been shot, on another November day. My father had loved JFK, as he called him, and was proud we'd had an Irish president (though Mom used to laugh and say that it was only Kennedy's grandfather who was Irish). Dad had driven, alone, all the way from Chicago to Washington for the state funeral. All the way in our old, battered sky-blue automobile.

I remember vividly when he came home. Dad was really upset, something I'd never seen before, and he stood in the kitchen telling Mom all about it in a soft, strained voice.

'It was sunny but very cold, and I was standing on 17th Street, waiting for a long time. There were thousands and thousands of people all lining the streets as far as the eye could see.

'Then I heard the muffled sound of drums. Such a terrible beat, Kathleen. Getting closer and closer.

'Then the funeral cortege passed. They'd laid the casket on a gun carriage drawn by six grey horses. Covered by the Stars and Stripes. A riderless black horse followed, then thousands of people, all silent.

'I wanted to follow as well and get across the river to Arlington, but I couldn't because of the crowds and barriers. I got as far as Memorial Bridge and waited along with everyone else.

'Suddenly there was a noise like thunder. People looked up and saw wave after wave of fighter aircraft flying by in V formation. The ground shook with the roar of it. Then scores of Navy planes passed overhead. And, last of all, Air Force One, the President's plane ...'

Then I heard another roar.

The roar of waves.

I threw the bike at the side of the track and ran down to the sandy beach where my dad used to swim. I stopped at the water's edge, staring at the thunderous procession of huge waves. The tears were hot on my cheeks and though I cried out loud I could scarcely hear myself above the storm.

The astronauts were going home, I was going home but Dad would never come home. It had taken me four years to really feel what that meant.

He would never come home.

The beach was empty but I didn't care if anyone else was there. I didn't care if anyone heard me as I called out to him, or if anyone saw me down on my knees tearing up the wet sand in my fists, rubbing it into my face and hair.

How long I sat there, I can't be sure.

There was one thing I had to do before I left. One last thing.

I stood up and stared at the waves.

Each one was a monster, a roaring bull of grey-green water intent on attacking the shore. The centre of each wave surged with awesome power. I was ready to tackle one of these giants, at last.

I changed into my swim shorts and put on my fins. Yet, even then, I stood back pondering the waves. You'd be a fool not to. If you wanted to ride on the bull's back, you'd better figure out how to get up there first.

I walked to the sheltered end of the cove. From here, I entered the water.

From the moment I dived in to evade the frenzy of white water thundering towards me, I knew I was in the right place. The shock of water washed the sand off my face and hair. It washed everything away.

I breast-stroked towards the next one and ducked again. Once more I felt and heard the powerful rush of white water over my body.

As I edged out further into the eye of the storm I suddenly found myself staring at a wave the size of the Great Wall of China. It swept towards me, rising, rising, preparing to topple. If I hadn't been a confident swimmer, if I hadn't been wearing my swim fins, I'd have been really worried. Stretching my arms forward, I dived cleanly under it. The great mass of water detonated just beyond me.

Once I emerged on the other side, there was time to swim out a bit and prepare for the next beast rolling in.

I noticed that every five minutes or so one wave would rise further out, bigger than the rest, and would kick towards shore. These waves were so high that they began to crest early, yet they moved with such speed that the crest could not break. Instead, the wave raced forwards, intact, and engulfed the shore in a deafening cataclysm.

One such wave was coming now.

As it bore down on me, I turned and swam frantically. I felt this enormous surge picking me up with the force of a rocket and carrying me away. Stretching out my arm, I kicked my fins and angled across the face of the water.

All other sounds of the sea died away. Only the rumble of this wave filled my ears, a sound that rose and deepened as we charged towards shore. From the corner of my eye, I saw the wave break on my right. I was at the point of no return.

The wall of green reared up into the air and a spinning tube of silver shot out and engulfed me from above; I was sucked into a vortex, certain I'd be whipped around and brought under.

I wasn't. I shot out the other side of the tube – clear, but only for an instant. All at once I was pounded into the boiling white water, still rocketing forward.

I stretched out my arms and became a human torpedo, shooting through crazy white-water rapids.

Then without warning, I was beached. Just like that, I was thrown up on the sloping shore. To say I came to a shuddering halt would sum it up. I struggled to my feet as the next wave rolled towards me.

Grazed by the sand, my stomach was red and sore. I hadn't expected such a sudden and painful end to the ride. The water had gone up my nose and invaded my ears. My hands were blue, my body numb with the cold.

But it was worth it a thousand times.

I had no wish to go back in again though. One monster wave was enough. I ran briskly down to the end of the small cove and back again to warm up.

The beach had been empty, but now I saw a man climb down over the rocks at the far end where the stream spilled out of the gully. He was tall and well built, with broad shoulders. He wore a white bomber jacket, a black cap and sunglasses. The cap looked Irish; the jacket and sunglasses American. Crossing the sand, he waved to me – a kind of salute – and I waved back. He strode up the dirt track and went out of sight.

Before cycling home, I called in to my Dad's parents to say goodbye. They gave me tea to warm me up, and thick slices of homemade brown bread. I told them Mom and Lucy would drop by tomorrow to see them, because we were going home, back to America, the day after. When it was time to leave, my grandmother hugged me tightly, and my grandfather clasped my hand in his big fists.

I took it easy on the way back.

As I coasted through the village, Lisa, the shop lady, came running out. 'Come here, come here!' she called breathlessly.

I stopped in the middle of the street.

'Did you see him?' she asked, eyes wide.

'See who?'

'Himself!'

'Who's himself?'

'Robert Mitchum, of course! Sure didn't he walk by here only five minutes ago,' she said, pointing down the road. 'If you hurry, you'll catch him.'

'Thanks,' I said.

'Do you want a pen and a piece of paper for his autograph?'

I thought for a second. 'Okay,' I said.

She ran inside, came back out and shoved a postcard and pen into my hand. 'Here, hurry up with you.'

As I cycled away, she called after me: 'He's in a white jacket – sunglasses – you can't miss him.'

I went as far as the fork in the road past Grandpa's place but there was no sign of him, or anyone else for that matter. I didn't mind. Still straddling the bike I stopped and listened to the breeze as it moved through the grass, just thinking.

42

I woke with sunlight streaming through my window. Across the little bay, Mount Brandon was clear, as if it had stepped out of the clouds again to say goodbye.

'How do you feel about going home tomorrow?' asked Mom, as I nibbled toast over breakfast.

'Good,' I said.

'I don't want to go home,' Lucy announced. 'I want to stay with Grandpa.'

'I know,' said Mom. 'But when you go home you'll be starting school and you'll have lots of girls and boys to play with.

'I don't *want* to play with boys.'

'Why not?' asked Mom.

'Because I don't want to kiss them.'

'You mightn't want to kiss them now,' said Mom, and she smiled at me, 'but you might want to kiss them when you're older, you know, later on.'

'I won't want to kiss boys when I'm five either,' Lucy answered firmly.

Mom and I laughed. Lucy was herself again.

A while later there was a knock on the door. It was Eilis, holding an apple pie that her mom had baked. It was still hot, and the smell was delicious. 'We want to fatten you up before you go home to America,' she said, placing the apple pie on the table. 'There you are now.'

'Eilis, thank you so much,' said Mom. 'Tell me, how's your father this morning?'

'He's grand, not a bother. The arms are a bit swollen, that's all,' she said.

'Yum, yum,' said Lucy, staring at the pie.

'Would you like a slice?' Eilis asked.

Lucy nodded enthusiastically and stuck out her tongue pretending to lick the apple pie.

'What about you guys?' Mom asked me. 'Like some?'

'Later,' I said.

'Maybe later,' agreed Eilis.

'Have you two got plans?'

'Only the bikes,' said Eilis.

'Then it's the *céilí* later,' I added.

'Well, it's your last day so you may as well enjoy it,' said Mom.

Eilis and I looked at each other and put on sad faces.

We rustled up sandwiches for a picnic and set off around midday. We stopped first in the village to give Lisa back her pen and buy some soda pop.

'Well, did you catch up with himself?' Lisa asked me.

'Afraid not,' I said. 'And today's my last day.'

'Ah, we'll miss you,' she said. 'But you'll have to visit us again.'

'I will,' I said.

She leaned over the counter and whispered, 'Tell me, are you two eloping together or what?'

'Sshhh,' said Eilis, putting a finger to her lips.

'My lips are sealed,' said Lisa.

'But we might come back for the *céilí* tonight,' I added.

'Oh, you can't miss that,' said Lisa. 'You can't miss that.'

We cycled out the road, the same one I had travelled the day before. We eased along, taking turns singing songs. Eilis would sing one in Irish and I'd follow with one I knew from back home. There was one we both knew, and we sang it at the top of our voices.

'Come on the sloop John B
My grandfather and me
Round Nassau town we did roam
Drinking all night, we got into a fight
We feel so broke up, we want to go home.

So hoist up the John B's sails
See how the main sail set.
Send for the Captain ashore, let us go home
Let us go home, let us go home
I feel so broke up, I want to go home.'

We passed by the side road that led down to my grandparents' house and were soon standing on the pedals and climbing steeply. I looked over my shoulder and saw the cove, way below, with huge waves rolling in.

Soon we had to get off our bikes and push them to the top of the road. A couple of cars were parked on the bend and tourists were taking photographs – I could understand why.

'If you think that view is go ' wait till you walk up there,' said Eilis, pointing to the craggy h lland jutting into the sea.

We left the bikes at the side of the road and made our way up.

'If you keep your eyes open, you might find some Kerry diamonds,' she told me.

'What are they?'

'Diamonds, you fool,' she replied, nudging me. A few moments later she pounced and picked up a small white rock. 'There, take a look at that.'

In the heart of the rock, a cluster of what looked like cut glass twinkled. 'There's your Kerry diamonds,' said Eilis, 'though a scientist might call them quartz crystals instead.'

'Cool,' I said.

'As far as I'm concerned, they're diamonds,' she added.

'Me too,' I said. 'They're beautiful.'

'Well, put that in your bag and bring it back to America,' she said.

We sat up on a high rock, like a king and queen surveying our kingdom: the pyramid mountain, Mount Brandon and the Three Sisters on one side; the islands, the peak of Mount Eagle and the glistening ocean on the other – all resting under the vast blue dome of the sky.

'This headland is named after a warrior called Diarmuid,' said Eilis. 'He fell in love with a princess called Gráinne. But Gráinne was already engaged. She was supposed to wed the chief of the warriors, an old man called Fionn whose wife had died recently. Anyway, she changed her mind and stole away with Diarmuid ...'

'So they eloped too,' I said.

'Yes, and Fionn and his men went after them,' she continued. 'Diarmuid and Gráinne hid in caves, forests and on mountains the length and breadth of Ireland. And right here –' she slapped the rock with her hand – 'is one of the places they visited.'

'Were they caught?' I asked.

'Not exactly,' she said. 'Fionn eventually gave up the chase. Diarmuid and Gráinne settled down and had children together. But one day, Diarmuid went hunting a wild boar and was gored by it. Now, there was only one person with the magical powers to save his life, and that was Fionn. All Fionn had to do was give Diarmuid a drink of water from his cupped hands and Diarmuid would be saved. Twice, Fionn went to the stream. Twice, he let the water run from his hands to the ground rather than heal his enemy. Fionn's son, Oisín, became so angry that he pulled his sword and told his father that he'd kill him if he did not go to the stream again ...'

'And did he go?' I asked.

'He did,' she said. 'But by the time he returned with the water, Diarmuid had given up his last breath.'

'That is one sad story.' I sighed.

'It is,' said Eilis. 'Now let's be off.'

When you come to the top of a hill, you go down the other side. That's what we did, freewheeling to the sound of our dizzy wheels.

Eventually, after many twists on the road, we reached a tiny beach. Spreading out our jackets we picnicked, lazing in the sun and gazing at the shifting waves that drew in and out of the cove. A stream also ran down off the rocks and into the sea. We, too, cupped our hands and drank from it. The cool water killed our thirst far better than any soda pop would.

'I'll write you from America,' I shouted over the roar of the sea.

'And I'll write back,' she cried.

'That'd be nice,' I answered.

She gave me one of her crafty looks. 'But you'll probably be so busy surfing with your friends and chatting to all those pretty American girls that you'll forget to write.'

'No,' I protested. 'It's far more likely you'll be so busy riding your crazy horse and going off to *céilís* and chatting to those Dublin boys you won't even open my letter.'

'Did you call my horse crazy?'

'He is crazy and so are you.'

She scooped up a handful of water in her hands and sprayed me with it. 'Take that!'

I filled my cupped hands and chased her over the sand.

It was some hours before we got back home. Our tour had taken us in a slow and winding circle around the mountains. We sat in the kitchen and helped ourselves to what was left of the apple pie and cream. Grandpa joined us, ladling extra sugar onto his pie.

Eilis was about to leave when I heard the front door open. Suddenly Sean bustled into the kitchen. 'Will you look what I just found!' he exclaimed.

My jaw dropped so far it almost hit the floor.

'What do you think? And it's stuffed and all!' he said, proudly holding up the muddy fox for all to see.

A four-dimensional silence filled the room.

I looked at Eilis; she looked at me.

Mom, shaking silently, crouched as if trying to hide under the table.

Grandpa cleared his throat and had a half-smile on his face.

'What do you think of that, boys?' said Sean. He stuck his finger into the bullet hole in Rowdy's chest and pulled out some of the stuffing. 'A clean shot. Mind you, I think he was already dead when that happened –'

'Ah no,' Eilis cut in quickly. 'After your grandfather here shot the fox, we had had it stuffed, didn't we, Danny? We wanted to stuff the fox to give it *you*, John – as a present. Isn't that so, Danny?'

Eilis, you're a genius, I thought. 'That's right, that's right,' I said, trying to swallow. 'After all, you shot the fox, Grandpa.'

Grandpa rubbed his chin and looked at me with those penetrating blue eyes. 'I thought you buried it. Did you not?'

'No,' I said. 'I just let on I did.'

'Is that so?' My grandfather slowly got to his feet, stretched and yawned. 'Is that so?' He paused and looked at me. 'Well, I'm not as green as I'm cabbage-looking,' he said and with that he walked out of the room.

At that point, Mom cracked up completely and Eilis fell into hysterics too.

'What does he mean by that?' I asked.

'"I'm not as green as I'm cabbage-looking?"' Mom repeated slowly, smiling. 'What do *you* think he means?'

43

I thought it best to steer clear of Grandpa for a while. We packed our suitcases and tidied the bedrooms. Thanks to that, I was late getting to the *céilí*. Again.

Once more the hall was packed. A new crowd of students had arrived from Dublin and Eilis was dancing with one of them when I stepped inside. That didn't bother me, though. It didn't bother me because, come hell or high water, I was going to get the next dance with her.

When the music ended, the dancers parted like the waters of the River Jordan, the girls streaming to one side, the boys to the other. When Eilis sat down, I saw her smile and wave to me. I waved back from No Man's Land near the entrance.

Then I thought, *Guess what, Danny, rules are made to be broken. Besides, I'm from America. And this is my last day here …* I took a deep breath and walked across the empty dance floor. I didn't know whether people were staring at me or not but it felt as if they were.

I stood before her and said, 'May I have the next dance please?'

She giggled. 'You may but it hasn't started yet.'

I glanced over my shoulder at the band on the stage: the old woman was tuning up her fiddle; the man with the piano accordion and the kid with the tin whistle were sharing a joke.

'Do you come here often?' I asked her.

'I do and I'm always on time too,' she replied with a raised eyebrow. 'Will you sit down?'

Before I could answer, she turned to the girls on either side of her. 'Will you two shove over and make room for this rascal from Florida?'

The grinning girls created a space on the bench and I sat myself down – or, rather, squeezed myself in.

'Now, you keep your hands off him, Mary,' said Eilis, 'and I'm warning you as well, Sarah.' She pointed a finger at my chest. 'And you, mind yourself!'

The girls were greatly entertained at this. As for me, I wished that music would start up again soon.

A minute later it did, and we stepped out on the floor.

At a *céilí* you don't just dance with one person, you dance with everyone. And that's how it was that night. We stepped through the Walls of Limerick and the Siege of Ennis again, and this time the two of us danced the sets together, with Eilis leading the way. I figured that with a little more practice I could get the hang of it all.

But time flies when you're having fun and, before I knew it, we had arrived at the final dance, the old-time waltz. She and I took up a position on the floor waiting for the band to begin.

'This is our last dance,' I said, as if she didn't know.

Eilis looked at me and was unusually quiet.

Then the 3:4 beat started up. We joined hands and away we went, gliding and turning, around and around the floor.

After that, we strolled homewards. The full moon was high over the mountain and you could see for miles and miles out on the silvery ocean. When the sound of the cars finally died away, the distant rumble of waves rose up from the shore.

We walked on, trying to chat about this or that or just walking in silence. For once neither of us really knew what to say. At last, reaching her gate, we stopped and turned to each other. I looked at her and thought, *Isn't she the loveliest girl in the whole wide world!*

'Promise you'll write,' I said.

She nodded. 'And you promise too.'

'Yes.'

She held out her little finger, I stretched out my little finger and we linked them.

And then I kissed her lightly.

As I made my way up Grandpa's bohereen, I could not tell whether I was the happiest or saddest boy in the whole of Ireland.

44

By 7 a.m. we were ready to leave. I stood by the open door of the car waiting for Mom to come out with the keys. Grandpa walked over with Kerry at his heels and gave me one bone-crusher of a handshake. 'Will you come back to us?' he asked, looking straight into my eyes.

'I hope so, sir.' I paused. 'Grandpa, about that fox–'

'Forget about the fox,' he said with a gentle a wave of his hand. 'The fox is dead, boy.' He gave a sly wink of his eye. 'Or is she?'

I gave a short, nervous laugh.

Mom came out of the house, looking flustered. 'Okay, let's get moving … Where's Lucy?'

I pointed to my sister, who was playing over by the hedge.

'What have you got in your hand, Lucy?' I asked, as she seemed to be hiding something behind her back.

'Nothing,' she answered guiltily.

'Let me see,' I insisted.

She shook her head.

'Lucy, let me see,' I repeated.

She held out her closed hand. I could see part of a leaf sticking out.

'What have you in your hand, honey?' enquired Mom in a kind voice.

Lucy opened her palm. 'Ladybugs,' she said sadly.

'Wow, that's cool,' I said, staring at the two insects.

'What are their names?' Mom asked.

'Trudy and Judy,' whispered Lucy.

'Are you going to put them back now, honey?' said Mom quietly. 'We have to go.'

'I want bring them home to America,' she said.

'But you can't do that, darling,' said Mom. 'Trudy and Judy are Grandpa's friends and they would be lonely without him. And he'd be lonely too. Isn't that so, Grandpa?'

'Oh-ho, you could say that,' said Grandpa, staring out to sea. 'You could say that.'

Lucy handed the bugs to me and I rested them on the hedge. Then Mom gave her dad a tearful hug and I held up Lucy to kiss him goodbye. As the car rattled off down the bohereen, we waved and waved till he was out of sight.

45

We didn't win the space project. Neither did Bobby Schultz. That honour went to the girls – Linda Palmer and Gloria Romero. They had – wisely – turned down Jimmy's offer of joining our team, preferring to work on their own. It had paid off for them. As Mr Walker put it, they won the competition 'hands down, fair and square'.

Me and Jimmy didn't mind. We were happy for them. Though I have to say, the sight of Linda and Gloria carrying the Saturn V away and taking it home on the roof of Mr Palmer's car left us feeling a little green.

Anyway, Jimmy invited me down to his place in Daytona Beach that weekend and we quickly forgot our disappointment. We went surfing and caught ourselves a few waves. They were puny compared to the ones in Kerry, but I didn't tell Jimmy that.

Not long after I got back, I had written a letter to Eilis. And now I waited and waited for a reply. It sure can take a long time for letters to pass over the Atlantic and back. Finally, I arrived home from school one day to find a parcel waiting for me. Even if I hadn't seen the Irish stamps or the picture of a horse and the pair of shamrocks drawn on it, I knew who it was from. It was addressed to: DANNY SULLIVAN ESQ.

'I guess that's me.' I smiled at Mom.

I took it upstairs and opened it. Inside there was a bar of Cadbury's chocolate, a packet of Tayto crisps, a small bag of Bulls'-eyes, a long and very beautiful pheasant feather, some pressed blue, purple and yellow wildflowers and – this had to be for Lucy – a tiny doll dressed in the green and gold Kerry colours (Kerry, I was to learn, had just won the All-Ireland Football Final again – for the twenty-first time).

And there was a long letter.

I kicked off my shoes, sat up on the bed and started to read …

Also available from **Pixie Books**
www.pixiebooks.ie

The Irish Famine, by *Gail Seekamp and Pierce Feiritear*

(Age group: 10 years upwards)

"In the format of easy-to-read information bites, this well researched account of the Irish Famine is an excellent potted history." **Sunday Tribune**

Paddy the Pigeon, by *Gail Seekamp*
(Age group: 10-12 years)

…Read about the amazing World War Two adventures of this feathered hero – the only Irish animal ever to win a Dickin Medal for bravery…

"Gail Seekamp writes with a lovely sense of pace, a lovely sense of quiet humour and manages to resurrect both the feel of rural north Antrim and the World War Two battlefield … I love this book."
Robert Dunbar, children's books critic

Brush, A Tale of Two Foxes,
by *Pierce Feiritear*
(Age group: 7- 9 years)

"Animal stories for young readers don't come much better than this… Great fun."
Children's Books Ireland Magazine

For information and orders, please contact:
Pixie Books 21 Cherrymount Park, Phibsboro, Dublin 7, Ireland. Tel: (353) 1-838-4224 Email: info@pixiebooks.ie
Web: www.pixiebooks.ie